D0856212

THE WORLD OF TIM FRAZER

Tim Frazer's friend and ex-business partner Harry Denston has gone missing. That's not all—he owes money and there are several people desperate to track him down.

Tim Frazer's pursuit involves cars and boats and various characters, but he manages to survive while others around him perish. A Russian ship has just been wrecked off the Yorkshire coast and a man from the boat dies in a local hostelry.

Yet Frazer eventually becomes enlightened as the various clues are pieced together.

THE WORLD OF
TIM FRAZER

Francis Durbridge

SEO Library Center
State Library of Ohio

40780 Marietta Road, Caldwell, OH 43724

First published 1962
by
Hodder & Stoughton

This edition 2002 by Chivers Press
published by arrangement with
the author's estate

ISBN 0 7540 8605 4

British Library Cataloguing in Publication Data available

Printed and bound in Great Britain by
Bookcraft, Midsomer Norton, Somerset

THE WORLD OF TIM FRAZER

CHAPTER ONE

I swung the car into one of the middle traffic lanes of the M1 and put my foot down hard. As the finger ticked over eighty I settled back to enjoy the exhilaration of the speed, but it was not long before I started brooding over Harry Denston again.

It was over twelve years since I had first met Harry when we were engineering students at Birmingham University, rushing out at the end of lectures to the nearest pub, where Harry always drank single or double whiskies, according to the state of his finances at the time. I was always content with beer.

In the course of a few months it became obvious that an engineering works was not a very appropriate setting for the charm and happy-go-lucky nature of Harry Denston. I was not surprised to hear him announce one evening that he was joining the R.A.F., where he hoped to find a bit more excitement.

Harry was obviously much more at home in the R.A.F. and I was soon hearing reports of his rapid promotion. In a couple of years he had achieved a commission. So I was a little surprised, a year later, to meet him by chance in Regent Street and to see him in plain clothes. Harry was the type who enjoyed wearing a uniform at every opportunity, especially when it was an officer's.

He seemed highly delighted to see me again and insisted on standing me several drinks at a Victorian pub behind Oxford Circus. It was at least ten minutes before he admitted that he was no longer in the service; it appeared there had been some sort of "misunderstanding" about the mess accounts. But he laughed it off quite convincingly, declaring that there was nothing for him in the R.A.F. in peacetime.

Under the influence of the drinks combined with Harry's sunny charm I was foolish enough to tell him that I had just inherited the family's small engineering works at Hornsey from an elderly cousin who had just died. His eyes lit up at once, and he seemed full of sympathetic interest. In vain I tried to assure him that the firm was overdrawn to its limit, that the plant was out of date, and that the entire staff consisted of four workmen, two apprentices, and a typist-clerk.

There was no deterring Harry.

"You've got the potential there," he kept assuring me. "All you have to do is bring the outfit up to date, get some new plant, branch into some of the more modern lines, like plastics. I was talking to a chap only yesterday, who was looking for somebody to turn out a hundred thousand plastic bags for an airline."

Harry always knew somebody who was looking for something or other. Anyhow, before the pub closed Harry had persuaded me to take him into partnership. He was supposed to put in a thousand pounds, but that never materialised, although he airily assured me that he would have no difficulty in raising it.

Strangely enough, the partnership was quite a success for a time. Between us we managed to inject a considerable amount of new life into the old firm. Harry saw the bank manager and persuaded him to extend our overdraft so that we could buy several new machines. It was Harry who landed us orders for all sorts of novelty lines that showed a good profit. It was Harry who went abroad and explored the field over there, bringing back a couple of orders from West Germany that kept us busy for over six months.

Sometimes it was by no means easy to fulfil some of the orders that Harry accepted, but that was my headache, and we usually managed to deliver on time. At the end of eighteen months we had doubled our staff and floor space and reduced our overdraft to a mere eight hundred. Outwardly, the picture was pretty rosy, but I had already begun to entertain certain qualms on Harry's account.

Unfortunately, Harry never seemed to be happy unless he was living beyond his income, and in no time he was playing the part of the business executive, complete with expense account and a Hillman Minx. He began making more trips abroad, and once or twice I discovered that he had been visiting the Riviera when he was supposed to be in Switzerland.

Back in London, he spent far too much time in night clubs. In one of them he caught Helen Baker, the West End actress, on the rebound from her divorce, and they had only known each other for a couple of hectic weeks when they announced their engagement.

I did my best to restrict Harry's expense account, but it was by no means easy, and the accounting side of our business was the least efficient. I had too much on my hands in the works to spend much time in the office, and had to leave most of it to an elderly cashier who was terrified of offending Harry.

However, as the orders continued to flow into our books I was content to concentrate upon practical matters, and Harry went his own sweet way, giving the impression to most of our customers, I learned later, that he was the boss of the concern.

It was not until the end of our third year together that the company's accountant took me aside one morning and showed me half a dozen cheques which had obviously been worrying him considerably. They were for quite large amounts and had been cashed by Harry at various banks. They bore his own signature and mine as usual, and were apparently in order. It was not until I examined them closely that I realised my signature had been forged. It was a very good forgery.

Naturally, I had to have a showdown with Harry Denston.

He began by denying it, as I expected, but when confronted with the question of what goods or value had been received for the cheques he eventually broke down and admitted that he had drawn them to pay off a few urgent debts. I guessed that they were not unconnected with gambling, but he was inclined to treat the whole affair quite airily.

"It's purely temporary, old boy. I'll pay it all back in a month or two."

"Now look here, Harry," I protested, "this isn't just a question of a few quid from the petty cash. It comes to nearly four thousand. What's more, you've never paid the thousand you promised into the partnership."

"Right, old man!" he nodded briskly. "Let's call it a level five thousand, shall we? Of course, Helen would let me have the money this minute, but I've got a big private deal on hand that should bring in ten thousand during the next few weeks."

"Private deal?" I queried suspiciously.

"Nothing to do with the business," he assured me hastily. "Just a ticklish job I'm putting through for a friend of mine."

He walked out of the office and I did not see him again for three days. Meanwhile, the bank was beginning to agitate about our overdraft which was now running pretty high, and on top of that two of our biggest creditors began to press for payment. One thing led to another, and at the end of the month we were facing liquidation. Harry Denston had been no help at all. He had been away for several two- and three-day spells, offering no explanations for his absences. I spent a lot of time trying to explain matters to creditors, but the big firms won't wait for their money nowadays, and two of our cheques had been dishonoured.

The day after our liquidation had been announced I had a note from Harry, scrawled on a half sheet of blue notepaper. It read: *Dear Tim, Our troubles are over. Meet me at the Three Bells, Henton, tomorrow afternoon. Will explain everything then. Yours, Harry.*

I left the M1 near Coventry and headed north-east.

CHAPTER TWO

I

THE A.A. Members' Handbook told me that Henton lies on the north-east coast of England, approximately midway between Bridlington and Hornsea, has a population of 368, and boasts no hotel that merits even one star. I racked my brains trying to think why Harry should want to meet me there but found no sort of solution.

Like most Londoners, I knew little about the north of England and was sure that Harry knew even less. Passing through Thorne I asked myself for the hundredth time why Harry should be in Henton, which I imagined to be a remote fishing village. Any fishing that Harry had done in the past had been in the South of France with a picnic basket, a cocktail shaker, and a glamorous companion within easy reach.

I took the A63 to Hull and then cut across country to Hornsea. A chilling wind was blowing in from the North Sea and I was thankful that the car had a heater. I switched on the radio for the six o'clock news, just as the announcer was giving out an item about a Russian ship that had foundered in the North Sea during the previous night, a few miles from Henton. "Two of the crew are known to have drowned," said the bulletin, "but the remainder were picked up and are now in Henton." I pricked up my ears at this; apparently Henton was on the map at last, but I was no nearer to discovering what Harry Denston was doing there.

I suppose that in the summer months Henton may lay some claim to being picturesque. As far as I could see at first sight it was a permanent target for the North Sea, which was battering at the harbour as if it hated every man, woman and child in the village. The wind was howling in from the sea: the sort of wind that bangs every unsecured door and sets window frames rattling. It was too dark to see any ships in the little harbour, but I imagined that they must be bouncing about like corks.

There only seemed to be one street, a mean and monotonous thoroughfare of unvarying two-storeyed houses. I soon found the Three Bells: it stands at the top of the street, near the small War Memorial, and at first sight seems almost too good for Henton. From the look of it outside I should have thought it merited at least one star in the A.A. Handbook. That, at least, was a pointer to Harry; he had always liked his comfort.

I parked my car in the courtyard behind the hotel and staggered towards the front door. The wind almost lifted me off my feet and I noticed it was tearing at the pub's swinging sign as if it were bent on wrenching it from its hinges.

The saloon bar was deserted, but it certainly looked a very presentable sort of pub. There was a cosy atmosphere, with a bright fire in an old-fashioned grate. The oak beams, bench tables and chairs looked both solid and tasteful. I began to feel a little happier about things.

There was a genial, well-built man behind the bar. He looked up as I came in and said cheerfully: "Good evening, sir."

I said: "Good evening. Are you the landlord?"

"That's me," he said, "Norman Gibson, at your service, sir. What can I do for you?"

"I'm looking for a friend of mine who's here. His name's Harry Denston."

"Staying here you mean, sir?"

"I imagine so."

The landlord looked bewildered. "There's no one of that name in my register," he said.

I stared at him. "But there must be. I had a letter from him, saying he was here."

He shook his head. "Must be some mistake, sir."

"Is there any other pub in Henton?" I asked.

Gibson wrinkled his nose disapprovingly. "There's the Crown," he said, "but they haven't got any letting rooms."

A sudden weak feeling of rage swept over me. I'd driven two hundred miles in answer to a letter from Harry, only to find that he wasn't there. To hell with Harry Denston, I thought.

I parked myself on a bar stool. I said: "Well, that's damned odd. A friend of mine wrote to me, asking me to meet him here."

"Best thing you can do is have a drink, sir," suggested Gibson sympathetically.

"You've got a point there," I agreed. "Make it a double Scotch and soda."

I felt a bit better after the drink, ordered another, and asked for a room.

"Certainly, sir," said Gibson. "For how long?"

I shrugged. "Two nights, possibly three. Will that be all right?"

"Yes," said Gibson. "Got a lot of luggage?"

I indicated my grip. "That's all."

Gibson said: "My daughter'll be along in a minute. She'll fix you up."

Outside, the wind continued to howl unabatedly. "You seem to have been having a bit of excitement round here," I remarked. "I heard about it on my car radio."

"Ah, you mean the Russian ship," said Gibson. "Shocking

affair. As a matter of fact, we've got one of the blokes off the ship here now. He's in a pretty bad way."

At that moment a girl came into the bar. She was plump, blonde, and pretty. She carried a basin of water and a towel on her arm.

Gibson said: "Hello, Madge. How is he?"

The girl shook her head dubiously and emptied the basin into the sink under the bar. She noticed me and tucked an errant curl into place. "Dr. Killick doesn't hold out much hope for him, I'm afraid," she said.

Gibson turned to me. "That's the Russian sailor I was telling you about," he explained. "Is the doctor still with him, Madge?"

"Yes, but he seems to doubt whether he'll last the night."

Gibson made a clicking noise with his tongue. "As bad as that, eh?" he said. "Poor devil, it's a shocking thing. I just can't get over it. Hasn't he come round again?"

Madge shook her head. "Not since last night. I think I'd better sit with him tonight, in case he gets any worse."

Selfishly perhaps, I did not give a great deal of thought to the Russian sailor; I had enough troubles of my own. But a solitary meal did quite a lot to dispel my mood of profound irritation: the steak was done exactly as I liked it and the vegetables might have been cooked by a Frenchwoman.

I had another drink in the bar and went up to my room at ten o'clock. I suddenly realised that after my two hundred mile drive I was extraordinarily tired. The problem of Harry Denston, wherever he might be, would have to wait until the morning. By half past ten I was fast asleep.

It must have been close on midnight when I heard the persistent knocking. I struggled out of a deep sleep, sat up with a jerk, and realised that the knocking was on my own door. I stumbled across the old oak floorboards and opened it. Outside, Madge, clad in a dressing-gown, eyed me fearfully.

"I'm ever so sorry to knock you up, Mr. Frazer," she said, "but could you come a minute?"

I said blearily: "What's up?"

"It's the Russian sailor. He's been taken terrible bad."

"What's the matter with him?"

"I don't know. I thought he was sleeping, but he suddenly opened his eyes and started talking. He got all sort of frantic and I didn't know what to do. So I knocked you up."

I put on my dressing-gown and slippers. "All right, Madge," I said, "I'll come and have a look at him."

She led the way to a room at the other end of the corridor.

The man in the bed was far gone in delirium. He was quite young, I noticed, and his black hair hung over his forehead in damp curls. His hands clutched at the coverlet convulsively and there was a frightening fixed stare in his eyes.

I had picked up a smattering of Russian in Germany just after the war, and I bent my head to try to catch what he was saying. Most of it sounded absolute gibberish to me, but I caught the words "sea" and "captain". Then suddenly he sat up and very distinctly said: "Anya! Anya!"

I eased him back on to the pillows and said: "Steady, old man, take it easy." He started mumbling again and I didn't understand one word in ten. Madge leaned over and wiped the sweat from his forehead. He seized her hand and muttered brokenly: "Anya, Anya . . ."

Madge freed her hand with difficulty and we got him back on the pillows again. Gradually his muttering stopped and his breathing grew easier. Then, quite suddenly, he slipped into unconsciousness, with a rapidity that seemed far from normal.

I said quietly to Madge: "We'd better leave him now, I think. There doesn't seem to be anything more we can do."

Madge nodded wearily. She said: "What time would you like a cup of tea in the morning, Mr. Frazer?"

"When you wake up," I told her. I looked at the Russian again; he moaned once and I thought he said "Anya" again, but I wasn't sure. We crept out quietly and went to our rooms.

I slept fitfully for the rest of the night. Twice I woke, imagining I could hear moaning, but when I listened there was nothing but the howling of the gale.

I had breakfast early and, feeling the need for fresh air and exercise, went out directly afterwards. The wind had dropped somewhat, but it was still bitterly cold. The lowering black skies told me that the storm had not entirely abated. As I walked down the narrow street towards the harbour I decided to give Harry another day, just in case he had met with some accident.

I was still feeling pretty sour about the way things had gone. If, as seemed highly probable, Harry didn't turn up, I was faced with the two hundred mile journey back to London: four hundred miles of motoring, two nights in a dreary little fishing village in the middle of nowhere, and not a damned thing to show for it. As I turned back from the saltings, with the wind whistling round my ears, I cursed Harry Denston once again.

That evening I sat in the saloon bar, deserted except for four fishermen playing cribbage in the corner. The wind had got up again and was howling with renewed fury. I drained my pint tankard and handed it to Norman Gibson for a refill.

"Wind hasn't dropped, then," he remarked.

"It certainly hasn't," I said, "although it wasn't too bad out this morning. I thought the storm was blowing over."

"Aha," said Gibson knowingly, "they don't go over that

easy." A window rattled and the landlord glared at it balefully. "Bloody thing," he said to no one in particular.

The door of the bar opened, bringing with it a gust of wind. A man came in and stood for a moment, breathing heavily. He did not cut an impressive figure. He was about fifty, with a receding chin and an untidy moustache. Drops of rain dripped from his bowler hat, and his shabby raincoat gave him the appearance of a rather badly tied brown paper parcel. He took off his hat, displaying thinning and wispy hair, the same colour as his moustache but plentifully streaked with grey. His luggage—a battered suitcase and briefcase with one strap broken—completed the bedraggled picture. He looked tired and oddly pathetic.

"God Almighty!" he gasped. "What weather!" His voice was high-pitched, ultra-refined, and catarrhal.

Gibson leaned over the bar, wearing an expression of professional welcome. "Good evening, sir."

"Don't know what's good about it," said the man morosely. "You the landlord?"

"That's right, sir. Gibson's the name. And what can I do for you?"

The man undid the top buttons of his raincoat, revealing a disarranged bow tie. "I'd like a room, old man," he said. He peered round the bar. "That is, if you've got any rooms."

"Just for one night?" asked Gibson.

"Yes. Possibly two, but I hope not." He gave a phlegmy cough and extended his hands to the fire. "Had a bit of a bust-up with the car, y'know."

"Reckon we can fix you up, sir," said Gibson genially.

The man took off his raincoat and advanced on the bar. The warmth of the room had restored some of his self-assurance and his voice was appreciably louder. "Now, all I need is a good stiff Scotch—better make it a double."

Gibson measured the drink. "Anything with it, sir?"

"Not likely." He picked up the glass and swallowed the whisky in a single prolonged gulp. "Let's have the other half and one for yourself, old boy." The whisky was working on him already and a slight flush suffused his veined cheeks. I sat watching him without enthusiasm: it was going to be a long evening and in my present somewhat jaundiced mood he did not strike me as being the ideal drinking companion.

Gibson took a half-pint tankard off a hook. "I'll have a beer if I may, sir."

"Whatever you like, old man," was the airy reply. He took a sip at his second whisky and smacked his lips appreciatively. "Nothing like a drop of the old highland fling." He turned to me. "What about you, old boy?"

"Thanks," I replied rather shortly. "I'll have a half of bitter."

He looked at me for a moment, sizing me up. He's wondering, I thought sourly, if I look the type who'll sit up half the night to provide an audience.

The man turned to Madge: "By the way, have you got a phone I could use?"

Madge nodded towards the telephone behind the bar. "Well, we would have normally, sir, but it's out of order at the moment. The storm blew the lines down."

"Oh, damn!" said the man. "That's all I need!" He drank some more whisky and tugged at his moustache with a petulant gesture.

"There's a call box just down the road," suggested Madge. "Their lines may be okay."

"No, I'll leave it," he decided. "Not important—it can wait." He looked round, obviously enjoying a captive audience, then turned back to Norman Gibson. "Now, what do I owe you, old man?"

B

"Two large Scotch, two small bitters—eleven and two-pence," said Gibson.

"Blimey!" said the man. "Still, never mind—it's on the old firm." He threw a ten shilling note, a shilling and two pennies on the bar and raised his glass. "Well, cheers, folks. I must say, you get some pretty rough weather in these parts."

"It's an improvement on last week," said Gibson.

The man laughed. "What did you have last week, a typhoon?"

"It certainly felt like it," said Gibson feelingly.

Madge made an effort to interest the newcomer. "Didn't you read about the Russians?" she asked.

The man halted the passage of his glass to his lips. "Russians?" he repeated. "They're always in the headlines. What have they been up to in these parts?"

"One of their ships got wrecked the other night," said Gibson with a note of reproof in his voice.

"Oh, yes, I read about it. So that was here, was it?"

"Just outside the harbour," nodded Gibson, "almost on our doorstep. Those lifeboat boys did a wonderful job." He shook his head portentously. "Worst storm I remember in thirty years."

"It's always thirty years," said the man with weighty condescension.

"You ought to have had a basinful of this one, that's all," said Gibson. He sounded almost possessive about the storm.

"Today's little lot will do me," said the man. He turned to Madge. "Did they get the men off all right?"

"They rescued most of the crew," said Madge, "but two were drowned—swept away."

"If you ask me, it's a miracle any of 'em were saved," said Gibson.

"Where are the ones that were rescued?" asked the man.

"In the Cottage Hospital," replied Gibson. "Although as a matter of fact we've got one of 'em here." He pointed towards the stairs.

"Really? How did that happen?"

"They had to bring three or four of them here while the rescue work was going on," explained Gibson. "This chap Anstrov was too ill to move. The doctor wouldn't have it, so here he is. Poor chap, it's touch and go whether he lives."

"He was in the water for hours," supplied Madge.

"Poor devil," said the man. "What a shocking experience." He passed a hand over his untidy hair and fingered his bow tie. With two double whiskies inside him he suddenly seemed to have increased in physical stature; clearly a saloon bar was his second home. "Personally, I like to keep both feet on dry land"—he turned to me—"don't you agree, old boy?"

"In this sort of weather, certainly," I said.

The man patted his stomach ruefully. "Feeling a bit peckish," he announced. "Haven't eaten anything since lunch. Think you could rustle me up a couple of sandwiches, m'dear?" He favoured Madge with his idea of a winning smile.

"Of course, sir," said Madge. "What about ham or tongue?"

"Just the job. Make it a round of each, there's a dear." He turned to me again. "My name's Crombie," he said, extending a hand.

"Tim Frazer," I said, accepting the moist palm.

"I'm from Leeds," went on Crombie, "in the old rag trade."

"The—er—what trade?" I inquired.

"The rag trade—textiles."

"Oh, I see," I said. "Are you just passing through Henton?" The man was obviously determined to make conversation and it seemed unfriendly to discourage him.

Crombie made a grimace. "Wouldn't stay here five minutes if I could help it"—he grinned placatingly at Madge—"all due respect to your village, miss, of course. No, the fact of the matter is, I had a bit of a smash-up with the old jalopy. Upset all my plans."

"Where did this happen?" I asked.

"Few miles back, on the main road. Took the corner too sharp and—whoosh!—slap into a ruddy great lorry."

"You're lucky to be here at all," I remarked.

"You're telling me, old boy. Made a shocking mess of the car, though. My worry is I don't know how I'm going to get to Nottingham tomorrow—got a lot of calls to make there."

I ordered fresh drinks. "Isn't there a train?" I asked.

"There's one at seven forty tomorrow morning," put in Gibson.

Crombie shuddered delicately. "No, thanks. Change at every station and take all ruddy day, I shouldn't wonder." He raised his glass to me. "Well, bottoms up, old boy. This is a hell of a place to get stuck in, but as long as the old grog doesn't run out I might as well make the best of a bad job." He leaned his elbows on the bar. "What's your line of business, if you don't mind my asking?" he inquired.

"Engineering," I replied briefly. I didn't see much point in telling this character that I'd recently gone out of business.

"Engineering, eh?" said Crombie. "A lot of development in that line, I hear." He bit into a sandwich with obvious enjoyment and ogled Madge. "These sandwiches are a bit of all right," he announced, his mouth not entirely empty. "Remembered to put the ham and tongue in, too."

Madge tossed her head. "Nothing stingy about me," she said.

"I'll bet," said Crombie.

I reflected that another hour of Crombie's company would be about as much as I could take.

"As a matter of fact," I said, because I did not want to discuss engineering, "I'm feeling pretty fed up. I drove all the way from London to meet a friend of mine here and he hasn't turned up."

"I say, that's a bit offside," said Crombie with heavy sympathy. "Damned inconsiderate, I call that."

"Old Harry Denston never was over considerate," I said.

Crombie fastened on the name with glee. You've only got to mention someone's name to this type of man and he thinks he knows him. He mentioned two Denstons, a Denison, and a Cranston in quick succession.

The voice of Madge providentially cut across these reminiscences. "Here's Dr. Killick," she announced. "I wonder how our patient is."

We all looked up as the doctor came down the stairs. Killick was about fifty, short and baldish; he wore the worried expression peculiar to overworked general practitioners in outlying districts.

The doctor looked at us all in turn, as if fervently hoping that we were all in sound physical condition, and sank wearily into a chair.

"Any news, Doctor?" asked Gibson.

"Nothing new, I'm afraid," said Killick wearily. "It's only a question of time now; I'll be surprised if he lasts the night."

Madge said: "Oh, Doctor, isn't there anything we can do?"

"We've done all we can," said Killick in a defeated voice.

"Hasn't he come round at all?" asked Gibson.

"No. I've given him an injection and—well, quite frankly, I hope he *doesn't* come round. He's really better off as he is."

Gibson nodded understandingly. "I expect you could do with a drink, Doctor," he said.

"I certainly could," said Killick. "I'd like a whisky and soda, please."

Gibson measured the tot of whisky and squirted in a little soda water. "I'm only sorry it had to happen here," went on Killick. He favoured Madge with an avuncular smile. "Although I could scarcely have had a more professional assistant, even at the hospital."

Madge looked at me quickly. "I wasn't very professional last night," she said apologetically, "I had to knock up Mr. Frazer here."

Dr. Killick looked at me inquiringly. I said: "I'm afraid I couldn't do very much. Madge knocked me up last night and asked me to go along and see Anstrov. She was a bit upset about it, I think. Thought he might get violent."

"It was silly, really," said Madge, "but I'd been sitting with him all the evening and then suddenly he opened his eyes and started talking."

"In Russian, I suppose," commented Killick.

"I suppose so," said Madge, "though it might have been double-dutch for all I know. Anyway, I couldn't make head nor tail of it, and he was getting sort of frantic, so I knocked up Mr. Frazer."

"I see," said the doctor. He turned a very shrewd and penetrating pair of eyes on me. "Could you make out what he was talking about?"

"He didn't say anything intelligible," I said. "He was delirious and not making a lot of sense."

Killick looked surprised. "So you speak Russian?"

"A little," I said. "I can understand it better than I can speak it. The only thing that did make sense was that Anstrov kept on calling for someone—someone called Anya."

"Anna?" said Killick.

"No, An-*ya*," I corrected. "I suppose she's his wife or girl friend."

"And that's all?"

"I'm afraid that's all I could understand," I said. "The rest was just nonsense—absolute gibberish. Could have been some dialect, of course."

"Well, thank you, Mr. Frazer," said Killick. "I was anxious to hear your version of it because both the captain and the first mate keep asking me about Anstrov."

"How are the sailors in hospital?" inquired Madge.

"Well, two of them died, as you know," said Killick. "The rest are doing well—most of them are only suffering from shock. The first mate and some of the others are being discharged tomorrow."

"And what happens to them then?" asked Gibson.

Killick shrugged. "They'll be whisked straight off to London, I imagine. We've had the Embassy people up here, fussing round them like sheepdogs and generally making rather a nuisance of themselves. The men are very friendly souls—when they're given the chance!"

Gibson nodded agreement. "They struck me as being very decent chaps. Plenty of guts, too."

Killick finished his drink and rose to his feet. He turned to me with a courteous bow. "Thank you for telling me what happened, Mr. Frazer," he said. "I'll notify the captain. And now, if you'll all excuse me, I'll just take another look at the patient."

As the doctor left the room the telephone at the end of the bar rang. Gibson answered it, and then turned to Crombie. "That was the exchange," he said. "The phone's working again if you still want to make a call."

"Good," said Crombie, "I'll get on to the garage and see how they're getting on with my car."

Crombie went to telephone and I sat in the bar for a while. I had a sudden unaccountable feeling that something strange was afoot in this little village. There and then I made up my mind to give Harry Denston one more day. I made the necessary arrangements with the landlord, then I saw Crombie coming back to the bar and hastily went up to my bedroom; the strong sea air had made me very sleepy.

2

The storm raged all that night, but by next morning the wind had dropped. It was still bitterly cold, but the sun was struggling to find a way through the lowering grey sky.

There was an atmosphere of gloom about the Three Bells, for Anstrov had died during the night. "A terrible thing," said Norman Gibson, sadly shaking his head. "First time it ever happened in my house to a foreigner." Madge, near to tears, seemed worried that the Russians death was a reflection on her nursing ability. She had gone into his room early in the morning and found him, in her own words, "horrible still and cold". Dr. Killick, accompanied by P.C. Muir, Henton's solitary police officer, arrived and between them they carried out the banal formalities that follow death.

For want of something better to do, I checked over Anstrov's belongings with P.C. Muir. They seemed pathetically few and were all stained and crumpled by the sea: a wallet, a wrist watch, a comb, a tie pin, a notebook, a cigarette lighter, and a pair of cuff links.

Looking oddly domestic without his helmet, Muir sat opposite me at a table in the saloon. Breathing heavily and writing laboriously, he was listing the articles in his official notebook as I read them out to him.

"One pair of cuff links," I announced. I scrutinised them closely. "Silver, I should imagine."

"One pair of silver cuff links," intoned Muir, licking his pencil.

I picked up the next article. "One comb, black; one wallet; one cigarette lighter."

Muir wrote busily and then closed his notebook. "That the lot?"

I nodded.

"Not much, is it?"

"What happens to these things?" I asked.

"I dunno, sir," said Muir. "The captain's coming down later. I suppose we hand 'em over to him for this bloke's next of kin."

Arthur Crombie came down the stairs. He carried his suitcase and briefcase, and his raincoat was over his arm. He was freshly shaved, but was bleeding profusely from a cut on the chin which he dabbed at ineffectually with a not over clean handkerchief. His suit looked as if he had slept in it and his bow tie was wandering towards his left ear.

He raised a nicotine stained finger in greeting. "Morning," he said. "Been any phone calls for me?"

"Not that I know of," I replied.

"Damn and blast," said Crombie tersely. "That confounded garage swore they'd give me a ring." He blinked his bloodshot eyes and lit a cigarette. "These garages are all the same: promise to do a job and then sit on it for a week."

"Is the car supposed to be ready?" I asked.

"Well, they said they'd patch it up well enough for me to get to Nottingham."

"Why not give them a ring?" I suggested.

"Think I will," said Crombie. His eyes alighted on the

articles on the table. "Hello, what's all this lot? The Russkie's?"

P.C. Muir seemed to be wearing an expression of guarded disapproval. "That's right, sir," he said.

Crombie shuddered. "Fancy dying in a dump like this. Bad enough living here, I should think. Seen the landlord anywhere?"

"He's gone to the station to meet the London train," I told him.

"Mrs. Gibson's been visiting her married sister in London," supplied Muir.

"What about the daughter?"

"Out shopping," said Muir. "Said she'd be back in about an hour."

"Oh, hell!" said Crombie petulantly. He drew a smoky breath and turned to the policeman. "Well, since you seem to be the expert on local information, Constable, perhaps you could tell me what I do about paying my bill." His manner seemed to me to be unnecessarily aggressive and unpleasant. I felt a mounting sense of irritation.

But presumably P.C. Muir had met so many men like Crombie that they no longer annoyed him. He said affably: "Certainly, sir. Mr. Gibson left it on the bar, in case you wanted to settle up."

Crombie glanced at Muir, as if scenting impertinence. He opened his mouth to say something, changed his mind, and picked up an envelope from the bar. He slit open the envelope and looked at the bill with a jaundiced eye. "Blimey!" he exclaimed, "anyone'd think I'd had the flippin' bridal suite."

A car stopped outside, doors slammed, and Dr. Killick came into the bar. He looked, I thought, tired and depressed. He was accompanied by a large, fair man wearing a somewhat crumpled blue uniform. In spite of this, and the fact that he walked awkwardly with the aid of a walking stick, there was about him an indefinable air of distinction and tough, nautical competence.

Killick smiled wanly at me and then turned to the policeman. "This is Captain Nikiyan, Muir. He's come to collect Anstrov's belongings."

"Got 'em all here, sir," nodded Muir. "Mr. Frazer an' me made out a list; all the captain's got to do is sign for 'em."

"Thank you, yes," said Nikiyan, eyeing the policeman shrewdly.

Muir produced a ballpoint pen. "If you wouldn't mind signing for them, sir."

Nikiyan scribbled his signature at the bottom of the sheet of paper. Muir collected the things together and handed them to the captain. As he did so, a large ticket fell on to the floor. I picked it up and looked at it.

"This can't be Anstrov's," I said.

"What is it, sir?" asked Muir.

"A garage ticket," I told him.

"A garage ticket?" queried Nikiyan in a puzzled tone.

"It's a kind of receipt," I explained. "You get one when you leave your car at a garage." I looked at the ticket again. "This one comes from the Marble Arch Garage in London."

Captain Nikiyan shook his head vehemently. "Anstrov never in London," he said emphatically.

"No, he couldn't have been," said Killick slowly.

"Well, it came out of his room," said Muir positively. "Brought it down meself."

"Most extraordinary," murmured Killick. "What on earth would Anstrov be doing with a London garage ticket?"

"Quite obviously," I said, "it wasn't his at all. Either it was Gibson's or it was left behind by someone who stayed in the same room. Anyway, I'll give it to Gibson when he comes in."

I took the ticket from Muir and put it in my wallet. Then I turned to Nikiyan. "Captain, the night before Anstrov died he was conscious for a few minutes. I don't know if the doctor has told you this?"

"I haven't," said Killick. "But go ahead, Frazer. Tell him what happened."

Nikiyan eyed me, wearing an expression of polite expectancy.

"I went into Anstrov and he spoke a few words," I said. "All I could make out was that he was calling for someone called 'Anya'. That's all, I'm afraid. I just thought his family might like to know that."

"Anya," said Nikiyan thoughtfully; "that is perhaps his friend—his woman friend."

"Quite likely," I said.

Nikiyan nodded his head vehemently. "He was to marry a woman from Kiev. Anya is perhaps her name."

"I expect that's it," said Killick.

Nikiyan said: "Anstrov was a good boy. It is a tragedy to die so young—so very young."

"We're all very sorry, Captain," said Killick.

Nikiyan inclined his head. He sighed and shrugged his shoulders. "There is nothing we can do," he said sadly. "It is too late."

"Dr. Killick did everything he could, Captain," said Muir.

"*Da, da,*" Nikiyan interrupted him. "The doctor has been most kind. Everyone has been helpful"—he bowed with an awkward, jerky movement—"I wish to thank all of you for your kindness. You have been very good to us—all of you."

He shook hands with Killick, Muir, Crombie, and myself. He had a long, bony hand. Then Killick took him gently by the elbow and they went out together.

Crombie ruefully flexed his fingers, temporarily numbed by the force of Nikiyan's handshake.

"Extraordinary blokes, these foreigners," he said. "It's a wonder he didn't get the old vodka out while he was about it . . . "

3

I sat down to dinner that evening in a pretty black frame of mind. It seemed quite obvious that wherever I might eventually find Harry it wasn't going to be in Henton. Probably, I thought savagely, I'd find another picture postcard waiting for me in London, informing me that he'd just left Honolulu and would I meet him for dinner in San Francisco.

My thoughts turned to Helen Baker. I had seen her just before I left for Henton and under her assumed air of flippancy I could see that she was badly worried. I'm afraid I didn't feel as sympathetic towards her as I should have: any woman who contracted to marry Harry Denston should have her head examined.

I viciously skewered a portion of Mrs. Gibson's beautifully cooked cutlet. Harry, I told myself for the hundredth time, was a dead loss and when I next saw him I'd probably give him a damned good hiding. Even this line of thought proved unsatisfactory—I wasn't entirely sure that Harry, a middle weight boxer of some repute in his youth, might not give *me* a damned good hiding . . .

I decided to send Helen a telegram: almost certainly she'd be worrying herself sick by now. I scribbled the telegram on an old envelope and looked up to find Norman Gibson standing by my table.

"Did your friend get off all right, Mr. Frazer?" inquired Gibson.

"My friend?" I said, momentarily bewildered. "Oh, you mean Crombie. I wouldn't exactly describe him as a friend of mine. Yes, he left just before lunch. I'm off tomorrow myself, by the way."

"I'm sorry to hear that," said Gibson. "We were just getting to know you."

"I'm sorry about it myself," I said, not altogether accurately. "I was just writing out a telegram. Can I telephone it from here?"

"I'll get Madge to do it," said Gibson. "You have your coffee in peace." He called to Madge, who was repairing her make-up in the mirror behind the bar. "Leave the war paint for a minute and phone this telegram through for Mr. Frazer."

"The address is on the top, Madge," I said. "You'd better make sure you can read it."

"*Miss Helen Baker, Shaftesbury Theatre*," read Madge, then broke off in surprise—"O-o-oh! Is that *the* Helen Baker, Mr. Frazer?"

"The very same," I said.

Madge looked at me with something like awe; I had clearly gone up in her estimation. "Crumbs!" she said, almost with reverence. "D'you remember, Dad? We saw her in that picture when we went down to Leeds about a month ago."

"Oh, aye," said Gibson, who obviously was no film fan and didn't remember at all.

"She was smashing," went on Madge dreamily. "Ever so glamorous." She looked at me almost accusingly. "Is she a friend of yours, Mr. Frazer?"

"Well, she's engaged to a friend of mine." I almost added, "God help her!" but refrained just in time.

"Now, just get that telegram off and mind your own

business," admonished Gibson sternly. He turned despairingly to me.

"It's a bit of a scrawl, Madge," I said. "Sure you can read it?"

"She can read it all right," said Gibson. "Knows it by heart, I expect."

Madge shot a reproachful look at her parent and read: "*Returning tomorrow. No sign of Harry. Tim.* That right, Mr. Frazer?"

"Word perfect," I smiled.

When Madge had gone Gibson said: "Well, I'm sorry your pal didn't turn up."

"Can't be helped," I shrugged.

"Still, there's one thing," said Gibson, "you've had a bit of excitement, what with one thing and another."

"I suppose I have." Then I remembered the garage ticket in my wallet. "Oh, by the way—there was a garage ticket mixed up with those things of Anstrov's."

"Garage ticket?"

"Yes. But it obviously couldn't have been his, it was from a London garage. I assumed that it was either yours or that it had been left behind by whoever had the room before him."

I felt in the inside pocket of my jacket.

It was then that I discovered my wallet was missing . . .

CHAPTER THREE

I

I DROVE back to London positively seething with frustration. The loss of my wallet, which had contained forty-one pounds in notes, had been the last straw. Norman Gibson, of course, had been full of sympathy and had accepted a cheque in settlement of my hotel bill and cashed another for my travelling expenses: having regard to the state of my finances at the time, he was taking a bigger chance than he realised. P.C. Muir had been instantly informed, had taken full particulars, and assured me that he would investigate the matter at once. It would plainly take priority over out-of-date dog licences, cattle straying on the high road, and minor parking offences; they would all be contemptuously brushed aside until Mr. Frazer's wallet was recovered. As a result of this theft every Henton inhabitant would become a suspected criminal.

In more serious mood I considered my own unenviable position. I had been had for a sucker all along the line. I was out of business and pretty nearly broke. In the words of a popular song, I was bewitched, bothered, and bewildered.

As I took the main road to Doncaster I considered my tangible assets: one was the Ford Consul which purred so contentedly under my hand towards Nottingham—that should fetch at least seven hundred quid and would be the first thing to go. My comfortable mews flat would give place to a bed-sitter in Bayswater. I would have to draw in my horns until they were invisible. Alternatively, I could emulate Harry Denston and find a tame sucker for myself.

It was in this unpromising humour that, one hundred and twenty miles and many drinks later, I reached London.

I lost no time in becoming solvent again and sold the Consul for seven hundred and twenty-five pounds. The dealer had offered me seven hundred, but I stuck out for seven hundred and fifty. Eventually we agreed to split the difference after thirty minutes of pointless and high pressure chatter. I then took a taxi to my flat.

Mrs. Glover, my daily woman, was busy with her chores. She was a plump and motherly person who served me with an almost maternal devotion. I suspected that she thought it high time that I found myself a wife and settled down— sometimes I even thought so myself.

I noticed that the living-room was spotlessly clean and that Mrs. Glover had got in some fresh flowers. She paused in a determined onslaught with a duster on the mantelpiece and said: "Good evening, Mr. Frazer. Welcome home."

"Hello, Mrs. Glover," I said. "You're a bit late, aren't you?"

"I thought I'd pop in with a few flowers, sir," she said. "They do help to brighten the place up a bit."

I looked round the room. "Well, you certainly seem to have done that," I conceded. "How did you know I was coming back today?"

"I was here this morning when Miss Baker telephoned," explained Mrs. Glover. "She said she'd had a telegram from you."

I nodded absently and picked up a pile of letters, most of which were unmistakably bills. "It's very good of you to take so much trouble, Mrs. Glover," I murmured.

Always a garrulous woman, she seemed disposed to linger.

c

"I've brought you some tea and milk," she went on. "I think you should be all right now, sir."

"I'm sure I shall," I said. "Are there any messages?"

"Yes," she said, wrinkling her forehead as she recalled them. "A Mr. Ross telephoned—twice, as a matter of fact. Once this morning and again about ten minutes ago."

"Ross?" I queried. "I don't think I know anyone called Ross. Are you sure you got the name right?"

Mrs. Glover folded her arms deliberately. "Mr. Frazer," she said severely, "have you ever known me get a name wrong?"

"Never," I replied readily. "Did he say what he wanted?"

"No; he just said he'd phone back later."

At that moment the door bell rang. "That'll be Miss Baker," Mrs. Glover declared eagerly. "She said she'd probably pop in on her way to the theatre."

Helen Baker came into the room and Mrs. Glover made a discreet withdrawal. Helen looked tired and worried; she was pale and there were dark circles under her expressive eyes. Even her chestnut hair lacked its customary lustre. She said in an oddly flat and expressionless voice: "Well, Tim—how are you?"

"I'm all right," I said. "Would you like a drink?"

She took off her coat and threw it carelessly on to a chair. Then she held out her hands to the fire. "I'd better not before the show," she decided.

I moved towards the drinks table. "Mind if I do?"

I mixed myself a whisky and soda. Helen watched me for a moment, without speaking. Then she said dejectedly: "So he didn't turn up."

"No," I said.

She sighed. "I'm so sorry, Tim."

I drank some whisky and soda. "There's nothing for you to be sorry about," I told her.

She gestured impatiently. "But I feel responsible for the whole thing. Every penny you had was in that wretched firm."

I shrugged. "That's a slight exaggeration. Anyway, just because you're engaged to a man it doesn't make you responsible for all his actions."

She shook her head decisively. "Darling, I'm serious. How much did you lose? Ten thousand? Twelve?"

"Nothing like that." I put my drink down on the table and moved a little closer to her. "Helen, there's no point in going all over this again. I've really got no one to blame but myself, you know. When Harry started going off on these trips of his and neglecting the business I should have had it out with him."

"But you did have it out with him!" she said vehemently. "For God's sake don't come the injured martyr with me. You had a showdown with him and all you got was a lot of smooth talk." Her voice assumed a bitter note. "No one knows that smooth line of Harry's better than I do. Look at that letter he wrote you."

"Which one d'you mean, Helen?"

"You know damned well which one," she said heatedly. "The one that said *Meet me in Henton—all our troubles are over.* If you ask me, they're just beginning. I knew perfectly well he wouldn't turn up, and even if he had he'd have produced some crazy scheme to make you forget the money you'd already lost." She turned back to the fire again and tapped one foot impatiently on the carpet.

"You seem to forget," I said mildly, "that the firm was doing very well until—"

She wheeled round to face me again. "Until Harry messed the whole thing up—like he always does. The pair of you make me tired, with your old pals and 'we must stick together'

routine. Harry's had you for a sucker and you damned well
know it."

"Poor Helen," I said inadequately.

She gave a mirthless little laugh. "Poor Helen, nothing!
Poor Tim!"

"You know," I said in the same mild voice, "you've been
far more upset about this than I have."

Helen made a moue. "I suppose I have. But—well, you
haven't discovered your fiancé is just a 'con' man."

"You're still engaged to him?"

"Yes, God help me, I still am. Helen Baker makes a fool of
herself over a penniless, no-good, useless layabout like Harry
Denston." She laughed bitterly. "My press agent would have
kittens if he knew about this."

I looked at her for a moment. Then, without speaking, I
poured a large tot of whisky into a glass and added a little
soda. "I think you'd better have that drink after all," I
said.

Helen seemed to relax a little and took the glass. She said
listlessly: "I think you're right."

"I suppose you haven't heard from him?" I said.

"Not a word—not even a postcard. But he'll turn up. I
know Harry—it's all happened before. One of these days,"
she added darkly, "it's going to happen once too often.
Have you got a cigarette?"

I pointed to the box on the table. "Help yourself."

She lit a cigarette and smoked in silence for a moment.
Presently she said: "Tim, what are you going to do now?
Have you thought of starting up again on your own?"

I shrugged rather helplessly. "I don't know. I'm not
sure yet."

"Well, if you do, I might—" She hesitated and then went
on: "Well, I wouldn't mind putting up some of the money.

THE WORLD OF TIM FRAZER 37

After all, I've done pretty well lately, and I know it would be a good investment."

I held up a hand. "No, Helen. We don't do it like that."

"Why not? What d'you mean?"

"You know perfectly well what I mean. I'm not letting you repay Harry's debts—not under any pretext." I rested my hand on her shoulder for a moment. "Don't think I don't appreciate the offer, but I'm not thinking of starting up anything on my own. I've learned my lesson—"

"Learned it the hard way," interposed Helen sadly.

"Well, never mind about that. I'm not sunk yet. I may even go abroad."

"You shouldn't have much difficulty getting a job," she said.

I was relieved when the telephone interrupted the conversation.

The voice on the other end was crisp and cultured. "Mr. Frazer?"

"Yes," I said.

"Good evening to you," continued the voice. "My name's Ross. Sorry if I've disturbed you."

"You haven't. What can I do for you?"

The pleasant voice said: "I hope you won't think it's an impertinence on my part, Mr. Frazer, but I heard about your company going into liquidation, and I wondered if you'd made any particular plans for the future."

I pricked up my ears at that. "Well, no," I admitted. "I did have some vague idea about going abroad."

"I see. Well, if you should happen to change your mind perhaps you'd care to get in touch with me. I could use a man with your qualifications."

Somewhat taken aback, I said: "Thank you very much.

Perhaps you'd tell me the name of your firm and give me your telephone number."

There was a brief pause. Presently the voice said: "I think it might be better if you called in to see me here. I'd be delighted to meet you. Would tomorrow afternoon be convenient?"

"Certainly. Shall we say three o'clock?"

"That'll suit me admirably."

"The address is 29 Smith Square."

"I'll be there," I promised. "Thank you, Mr. Ross."

"Thank *you*, Mr. Frazer. Three o'clock tomorrow, then..."

Helen looked at me expectantly as I replaced the receiver.

"Good news?" she asked."

"There's no such thing," I told her.

2

Promptly at three the following afternoon I found myself in a large room, tastefully furnished in antique oak. A cheerful fire burned in the grate, and the only hint of austerity was provided by a large steel filing cabinet in one corner.

There were no fewer than four telephones on the ornate desk which matched the dignity of the room. Behind the desk were a number of roller maps which could be displayed in the same manner as one would pull down a blind.

Charles Ross rose from the desk, his hand outstretched. As we shook hands I studied him cautiously. At first glance he appeared very ordinary, if not nondescript. He could have been anything: a bank manager, a tax inspector, a lawyer, or a stockbroker. He wore a sober and well cut formal city suit, and was indistinguishable from a thousand other men in their early fifties who commuted daily to London.

"How nice of you to come, Mr. Frazer," he said cordially. "Do sit down and have a cigarette."

I said, "Thank you," and took a seat in a comfortable leather chair. Ross pushed a cigarette box towards me, then took a cigarette himself. As he lit it he regarded me thoughtfully through the smoke, and I found his very direct stare vaguely disquieting.

"I was sorry to hear about your company," he said at length. "You must have had some very bad luck."

"We certainly had our share," I replied non-committally.

Ross exhaled smoke towards the ceiling and leaned back in his chair. "I've got a proposition to put to you, Mr. Frazer," he announced. "It's rather an unusual one, but I think you'll find it interesting." He waited for me to speak.

"I'd like to hear it," I said.

"Perhaps I'd better explain myself a little more fully," went on Ross. "I'm in charge of a department—"

I interrupted him. "A Government department?"

"Yes."

So that was it. The civil servants wanted some know-how on the cheap. "I'm afraid I'm not really interested in working for the Government," I said, trying to sound polite.

Beyond a very slight elevation of his eyebrows Ross's face registered no reaction. "Really?" he murmured. "May I know why?"

"They don't pay enough," I said bluntly. There was no point in wasting time.

Ross examined his fingernails and eyed me with that faintly disconcerting stare of his. "In general, I agree with you," he conceded. "Civil Service emoluments on the whole are far from princely. But there are exceptions to that rule. My department is one of them."

I leaned forward. "Exactly what is your department?"

Ross did not answer at once. He drew on his cigarette and expelled a long stream of smoke.

Faintly irritated, I persisted: "Well, Mr. Ross—what is it? Don't tell me that you're the Secret Service!"

"That's a rather melodramatic description," said Ross, "nevertheless, I suppose it's as good as any. During the last war we tried to keep one jump ahead of Britain's enemies. The German Intelligence was good at times, but we like to think that ours was rather better. Unfortunately, Britain still seems to have enemies: we're trying to keep one jump ahead of them too. Perhaps our business could best be described as being nobody's business." Ross's smile was more friendly now, and he regarded me almost benignly.

"Are you M.I.5?" I asked, my curiosity now aroused.

"Not exactly."

"Then what are you?"

"I told you. We're a Government department. That description may not appear to be very illuminating, but we do have access to—er—certain funds that the tax-payer knows nothing about. We also have very broad—er—powers. Have I explained myself to your satisfaction?"

"No," I said rather rudely. "How do I know all this is true?"

Ross sighed gently. "On this desk you can see four telephones. Perhaps you'd care to pick up the second one from the right and ask for the Chief of the Special Branch. It's a direct line."

Feeling slightly foolish I picked up the receiver.

"Go on," encouraged Ross, "ask for Colonel Rolleston-Mann."

I shot a look at Ross, but his expression registered only sincere goodwill. I said into the mouthpiece: "Colonel Rolleston-Mann, please."

A man's voice said: "Just a moment please, Mr. Ross."

Presently another voice came on the line: "Hello, Charles. What's up?"

Ross took the receiver out of my hand. "How's the new grandson, Bill?" he said, and held the instrument so that I could hear the reply.

"Is that all you're ringing up about?" the voice on the other end inquired.

"That's all for now, Bill," said Ross.

"Well, buzz off," was the discouraging reply. "I've got work to do, even if you haven't." The Colonel rang off with a truculent click.

Ross placed his fingertips together and looked at me inquiringly. "Does that satisfy you, Mr. Frazer?"

"Yes," I said weakly. "What exactly do you want to see me about?"

Ross leaned back in his chair. "Mr. Frazer, you were recently in partnership with a man called Harry Denston. Apart from your business arrangement, I understand that Denston borrowed money from you from time to time."

"As a matter of fact he did," I said. "How did you know that?"

He flicked open the file on his desk and went on: "If my information is correct, you lost five thousand pounds in this business. Apart from that, Denston owes you—personally, not your firm—three hundred pounds." He closed the file and regarded me with perfect equanimity.

"Correct," I said, "but while you're about it you might add another forty-one pounds to that total."

It was Ross's turn to look surprised. "Another forty-one pounds?"

"Yes," I said. "Some days ago I had a letter from Harry Denston, asking me to meet him at a place called Henton—

it's up on the north-east coast. The letter implied that our business worries were over and that I was going to get all my money back." I shrugged. "He didn't turn up, and to crown it all I had my wallet stolen. There were forty-one pounds in it. I doubt if Harry stole it himself, but I thought I might as well put it on his bill."

Ross was smiling again. "Why not, indeed? I see what you mean."

"I'm delighted to hear it," I said with scarcely veiled irony. "Incidentally, it was a very nice wallet."

"Quite so," said Ross casually. "I've been admiring it."

To my utter amazement Ross took my wallet from his inside pocket and pushed it towards me. "I think you'll find everything quite in order," he murmured.

I picked up the wallet and checked through the contents. Everything was there. But there were still a lot of things that I had to know, even if Ross did have a direct telephone line to the Chief of the Special Branch. "I'm still a bit bewildered," said. "What exactly is this job you're offering me?"

A new voice, with a familiar ring, spoke from the doorway. "We want you to find Harry Denston for us."

I swung round. Standing just inside the door was a man I identified with some difficulty as Arthur Crombie.

At first I thought I must be mistaken, for this was an entirely different Crombie. Gone was the seedy, facetious, and shabbily dressed textiles representative that I remembered. This new Crombie had immaculately kept hands in place of the nicotine stained fingers and somewhat grimy nails that I had seen in the Three Bells. The straggly moustache had been clipped with military precision. The ultra-refined and catarrhal voice was now crisp and incisive; the voice of a man accustomed to command. (Crombie, I subsequently learned, had won the Distinguished Service Order in the early Western Desert fighting and spent the rest of the war in one of the less orthodox branches of Military Intelligence.)

I looked from Crombie to Ross in blank-faced astonishment.

"I think you know Crombie," said Ross. "He's a colleague of mine."

I blinked. "A colleague of yours?"

"Yes. We work together in this department."

I stared at Crombie, who grinned at me.

"I know I said I was in textiles, old man," he said, and once again I heard the nasal, snuffling voice of Arthur Crombie of Leeds. Then Crombie smiled pleasantly. "I expect you must have thought I was pretty ghastly. Incidentally, I'm sorry I had to take your wallet. I hope it didn't inconvenience you."

In spite of myself, I summoned up a wry smile. "Like hell it didn't," I said. I turned to Ross. "Are all your employees expert pick-pockets?"

"Some are better at it than others," said Ross lightly. "But Crombie is by the way of being our star turn in that direction." He went on more seriously: "I expect you think we're being unnecessarily mysterious, Mr. Frazer."

"I must confess to being a little confused," I said. "Exactly why did you get me here this afternoon?"

"We've told you why," said Ross quietly. "We want you to find Harry Denston for us."

"But Harry hasn't disappeared!" I exclaimed.

Ross raised his eyebrows. "Really?" he said. "Everything seems to indicate that he has." He looked at me with faintly frigid amusement.

"Well," I said lamely, "what I mean is, he's just gone off somewhere. Of course, you don't know Harry like I do. This sort of thing happened all the time when we were in business together. I never knew where he was from one day to another. He'll turn up sooner or later."

"We don't want him sooner or later." said Ross soberly. "We want him now."

"Have you tried to find him?" I asked.

"No."

"But why not?"

After a momentary hesitation, Ross said: "Because we have no wish to arouse curiosity in—er—certain quarters."

"But surely," I pointed out, "my inquiries will arouse a certain amount of curiosity somewhere."

Ross shook his head. "I don't see why they should. After all, you have a perfectly legitimate reason for wanting to find him: he was the direct cause of your business going bust and he owes you money."

"Which makes you the ideal man, from our point of view," interposed Crombie. "Besides, you know Harry Denston. You know his haunts, his habits, his friends—everything about him."

"I'm beginning to wonder just how much I *do* know about Harry," I said thoughtfully.

Ross leaned forward across the desk. "Do you want the job or don't you?" There was a new note of challenge in his tone.

"Aren't you taking a bit of a chance?" I said. "After all, you know practically nothing about me."

Ross produced a cold little smile. "Don't we, Mr. Frazer?" He opened a drawer in his desk and took out a manilla folder. "On the contrary, we know a great deal about you. Otherwise you wouldn't be here." He put the file down on the corner of the desk, in front of me. "There's your dossier," he said quietly. "Read it."

I read it. It was my dossier all right. After I'd finished

reading I put the file down on the desk and said, with what I hoped was a touch of sarcasm. "This is my Life, Tim Frazer."

"We try to be thorough," said Ross easily. Then he leaned forward and his voice became more incisive. "If you decide to accept this assignment we'll pay you double your previous salary and expenses. Well?"

I looked from Ross to Crombie in bewilderment. I could see that Crombie was smiling.

"I must have your decision now, Mr. Frazer," Ross said, "one way or the other."

I made up my mind quickly. "All right." I said. "I'll find Harry Denston for you."

"Good," said Ross.

With a slight feeling of irritation I came to the conclusion that there wasn't much change to be got out of this mysterious couple; they knew damned well I was going to say "yes" because they knew exactly how broke I was.

Then a sudden thought struck me. "You must tell me one thing," I insisted.

"Well?" said Ross.

"Why are you so interested in Harry? Why are you so anxious to find him?"

I saw Ross and Crombie exchange a quick look. Then Ross said: "Denston had an appointment with someone in Henton."

"Certainly he did," I said dryly, "with me."

"Not primarily with you, Mr. Frazer," corrected Ross smoothly. "You were invited to Henton merely as a cover for Denston's meeting with someone else."

"Who was this someone else?" I demanded.

"A man called Anstrov," said Ross.

"You mean the Russian sailor that died?"

Ross nodded. "Exactly. We think that Anstrov was meant

to be put ashore at Henton, but the shipwreck upset the plan and the rendezvous didn't come off."

"But I don't understand," I said. "Why should Harry want to get in touch with Anstrov? It doesn't make a particle of sense to me."

"We can't tell you that at the moment," said Ross. "However, find Denston for us and then we'll tell you."

"We have one clue, Frazer," said Crombie. "We think it's an important one. It's in your wallet."

I took out the wallet and looked through it. Then I held out the garage ticket. "You mean this?" I said.

"That's it," said Ross.

I turned to face Crombie. "So that's why you took my wallet."

Crombie nodded. "I've checked with the garage and found out that that ticket is for Denston's car."

I remembered Harry's car well: it was a Hillman Minx coupé. Harry had wanted to trade it in for a Jaguar and put it down against expenses for income tax purposes, but I had managed to dissuade him.

"Is it a Hillman Minx, GPD 297?" I asked.

"That's right," said Crombie. "It was left at the garage with the key just over a week ago. It was originally left for only one night; then the owner telephoned the garage to say it wouldn't be picked up for another week or so. They don't know Denston at the garage, they simply go by the ticket. You've got one half—the other's on the car."

I looked at the ticket. "I see," I said slowly.

"Our theory is that Anstrov had the ticket, just in case something went wrong and Denston didn't show up at Henton."

"In other words," explained Ross, "we think that Anstrov had an arrangement with Denston whereby if Denston didn't turn up Anstrov was to come up to London and pick up the car."

"And the car would lead him to Harry?" I hazarded.

"Exactly," said Crombie.

"But we could be wrong, of course," added Ross. This admission surprised me a little: they had been right about everything so far.

"It certainly seems to explain why Anstrov had the ticket," I observed. I took another look at it. " 'The Marble Arch Garage'—that's the big one near the Cumberland Hotel, isn't it?"

"That's right," said Crombie.

"Well, I've got the ticket," I said, "so I'd better start by picking up the car."

Crombie led me down a long corridor to a small room where an elderly, bespectacled and clerkly man sat at a desk, surrounded by filing cabinets.

"Evening, Henry," said Crombie. "This is Mr. Frazer. Make out a card for him and give him a hundred pounds to be going on with. He's with us, with effect from today."

The man called Henry nodded and went to a safe. From it he produced twenty five-pound notes. He then went to a card index box and produced a blank card. On it he wrote my name, address, telephone number, and age. "You might let me have a photograph of yourself in the next couple of days," he said.

I left the house in Smith Square feeling happier than I had for a long time. It struck me that Charles Ross ran a very efficient organisation.

3

I pushed open the swing door of the garage and went up to

the reception desk. The man behind it looked at the ticket, stamped it, and took an ignition key from a peg behind him. He pointed to a door just beyond the showroom. "You'll find the car through there, sir," he said.

Ten minutes later I was driving Harry's car in the direction of Oxford Street . . .

I turned into a side street off the Edgware Road and parked. I thought it might be a good idea to make a thorough search of the car, in the hope of finding something else to work on.

The map pocket yielded nothing except an A.A. Handbook and an old evening paper. I opened the glove compartment and took out a duster, an old race card, a pair of leather driving gauntlets, a pair of dark glasses, and a spectacle case. Inside the case I found a conventional pair of horn-rimmed spectacles, and on the inside of the lid a small label with a name and address on it:

Mrs. Ruth Edwards,
Talltree Cottage,
Cobham.

I sat frowning at the label for a few seconds. It could, of course, belong to one of Harry's girl friends: the old adage "Men don't make passes at girls wearing glasses" meant nothing to Harry—he'd make a pass at anything under fifty.

It occurred to me that Helen Baker might know who Ruth Edwards was. Newly engaged men, I know, sometimes rattled off a list of their previous girl friends to their fiancées—presumably with the intention of starting with a clean slate. I thought it unlikely that Harry would find such a precaution either necessary or desirable, but it was possible; with Harry anything was possible.

I crossed the street to a call box. I glanced at my watch and calculated that Helen should be in her flat. She answered almost immediately.

"Helen," I said, "I'm sorry to disturb you, but do you happen to know a woman called Ruth Edwards?"

She sounded mildly surprised. "Ruth Edwards? Rings no bell with me, darling. Should I know her?"

"I wondered if she was a friend of Harry's."

"Well, if she was, he kept very quiet about it."

"So you've never heard of her?"

"Never. But what—?"

"Thanks, Helen," I said quickly. "I've got to go now, I'm afraid."

"But Tim, wait! I'd like to know if this woman—"

"I'll explain later," I said. "See you soon."

I hung up and went back to the car.

I drove out of Esher and took the A3 for Cobham. I was beginning to realise what it must be like to be a detective: the endless routine inquiries; the infuriating succession of red herrings; the patient following up of each tiny clue, however vague it seemed.

Ten minutes later found me in Cobham. I stopped at a small general stores and inquired the way to Talltree Cottage.

"You can't miss it," said the woman in the shop. "It's got a pale blue gate and there's a tall tree just behind the garage."

It was easy enough to find. There was a small girl, about ten years old, playing with a ball in the garden. She was a rather serious-faced child with large, wistful eyes. From under her woollen cap appeared a long pigtail secured by a red ribbon. I said: "Hello."

The girl stopped bouncing her ball and looked up at me,

D

her features transformed by a sudden and oddly winning smile. "Hello," she said.

"Does Mrs. Edwards live here?" I asked.

She nodded.

We walked up to the front door together, and as I pressed the bell I turned to the child, who was regarding me speculatively. Her eyes, I noticed, were of a very dark brown.

"And what's your name?" I asked her.

With a strange touch of dignity, she answered: "My name is Anya . . . "

CHAPTER FOUR

I

I gazed into the large brown eyes that were studying me so curiously.

"Did you say Anna?" I asked.

"No, I didn't," replied the child with the utmost clarity, "I said *An-ya*."

It was incredible, I thought—it couldn't be a coincidence. For all I knew, Anya might be a common enough name in Russia and Eastern European countries, but it fell strangely on the ears in the heart of rural Surrey.

Before I could say any more the door was opened by a woman of about fifty-five. Her dark hair was tastefully styled and barely touched with grey; she was still handsome, though there was a hardness about her mouth and eyes. She looked at me in the distant manner with which housewives confront door-to-door salesmen and said: "Yes?"

"Are you Mrs. Edwards?" I asked.

"That's right," she said, still on guard.

I took the spectacle case from my pocket. "I'm sorry to trouble you," I said, "but do these belong to you?"

Mrs. Edwards looked at the case for a moment. Then her manner changed. "Why yes," she said. "I'd given them up for lost. I made inquiries all over the place with absolutely no result." I noticed that her expression had softened appreciably. She stepped aside and held open the door. "Won't you come in?"

Just before we went into the hall together Mrs. Edwards

turned to the child. "Anya! Time for tea, dear. Wash your hands in the kitchen."

So the child's name really was Anya.

"Come and meet my husband," invited Mrs. Edwards affably.

She led me into the sitting-room. It was large, low, and comfortably furnished with chintz-covered armchairs and chintz curtains. The ceiling had exposed oak beams which were used to display a small collection of well-polished brasses.

There was a predominantly nautical flavour about the room: there were two model ships on the mantelpiece and over it hung an oil painting of a schooner in full sail. Each of the four walls was covered with prints of sailing ships. I also spotted a ship's compass and an old-fashioned ship's barometer.

Mrs. Edwards led me to the open door of a smaller, adjoining room. It appeared to combine the functions of study and workshop and the nautical atmosphere, powerful as it was in the sitting-room, seemed all-embracing.

An elderly, studious looking man was working on a model ship on a rough wooden table. He wore disreputable dark grey flannel trousers, a rather shiny double-breasted blue blazer with dull brass buttons, and a woollen cardigan which appeared to be several sizes too big for him. I noticed that his black shoes had seen better days.

On all sides were model ships in varying stages of completion: there were sailing ships, steam ships, an ancient galley, and a replica of an old Mississippi paddle boat. A confused jumble of tools and a large book with a tattered leather cover completed the picture of disorganised industry.

Mr. Edwards blinked inquiringly at his wife and myself with mild and short-sighted eyes. Then he came towards us and into the sitting-room.

"Donald, I've got my spectacles back," announced Mrs. Edwards. "This gentleman very kindly brought them." She turned to me. "I'm afraid I don't know your name. This is my husband."

"Tim Frazer," I said.

I held out a hand to Donald Edwards and he shook it absent-mindedly. "What's that you said about spectacles, my dear?" he murmured.

"You know," said Mrs. Edwards, "the pair I lost in London about three weeks ago."

"Of course,"saidEdwards, "I remember." It was obvious to me that he did not remember at all.

"I can't tell you how delighted I am to get them back, Mr. Frazer," said Mrs. Edwards. "I've been completely lost without them."

"You've got your new ones," pointed out her husband mildly.

"Oh, yes—but they've never been quite the same as these, you know." Her look challenged him to contradict her.

"I didn't know," ventured Edwards meekly, "but I'll take your word for it."

Mrs. Edwards shot a reproachful look at her husband, and turned back to me. "Where on earth did you find them, Mr. Frazer? As far as I can remember, I left them in a little restaurant off Regent Street. I telephoned the next day, but they said no one had handed them in. Of course, people these days are quite incredibly dishonest."

"As a matter of fact," I said, "I found them in a car."

"In a *car*?" Mrs. Edwards' voice reached a high pitch of incredulity.

"Yes," I said deliberately. "It was lent to me by a friend of mine—a man called Harry Denston."

"Harry Denston?" repeated Donald Edwards. "I don't

think we know anyone of that name, do we, dear?" Looking at him, I was ready to swear that he was an absent-minded old man searching a memory that had long since proved unreliable.

Mrs. Edwards was no more helpful. "I don't think so," she said. "No. I'm sure we don't."

"He must have picked them up in the restaurant, or wherever it was you left them," commented Edwards.

"I suppose so," she agreed. "Did he ask you to deliver the spectacles to me, Mr. Frazer?"

"No," I replied. "As a matter of fact, I haven't seen Harry Denston for quite some time—not since I borrowed the car. I came across the glasses quite by chance, and as I was on my way to Farnham I thought I'd drop them in."

"How very kind of you," said Mrs. Edwards effusively. She turned to Anya, who had just come into the room. "Anya, look! These are the spectacles I lost. Mr. Frazer has brought them all the way from London."

"I'm afraid you've been to a great deal of trouble," said Donald Edwards apologetically.

"Not at all," I assured him. "If it had been out of my way I should have posted them to you."

"All the same, it was extremely thoughtful of you," said Mrs. Edwards. "I just can't tell you how grateful I am. My new pair is supposed to be exactly the same, but I don't think that new oculist is any good. I just can't get along with the pair he gave me."

Anya spoke for the first time since she had told me her name. "Is Mr. Frazer staying for tea?" she asked.

Mrs. Edwards laughed. "Yes, dear, I think that's the very least we can do," she said. "You will stay and have a cup of tea with us, won't you, Mr. Frazer?"

"Well . . ."

"I won't take 'no' for an answer," insisted Mrs. Edwards.
Edwards turned his mild eyes towards me. "That means you're staying," he said.

"Good, so that's settled." Mrs. Edwards took the child by the hand. "Come on, Anya. You can help me in the kitchen."

"Charming little girl," I said when they had gone.

"Yes, isn't she?" said Edwards. He looked almost wistfully, it seemed to me, in the direction of the kitchen. "A sweet child, and we're both devoted to her. I'm afraid we couldn't bear the thought of parting with her now." He broke off and peered at me through his thick glasses. "I expect you've got the wrong idea. Anya's not our daughter, you know."

"Oh, really?" I said inadequately. "I thought she must be."

"Oh, no. We have no children of our own. Anya's my brother-in-law's child. He's a widower, so she spends most of her time with us."

"I see," I said. The explanation seemed perfectly logical, but I could not rid my mind of this nagging doubt. I went on: "Anya—isn't that rather an unusual name?"

"I suppose it is," said Edwards. "Quite honestly, I don't know how she came by it."

"It's got a kind of Central European sound about it," I suggested casually. "Tanya—now, that's a Russian name. Anya might be Hungarian, or possibly Serbian. Certainly not English."

"Really?" said Edwards absently. "Of course, I know very little about these things. I remember she used to be teased about it when she first started school. Children can be cruel little devils, you know, and any child with an unusual name gets pounced on at once." He smiled reminiscently. "I remember going to school with a small boy called Horatio: his life was a perfect misery."

I quickly realised that further inquiries into Anya's ante-

cedents would get me precisely nowhere. The mention of
Horatio was a proffered nautical conversational gambit that
it would be positively boorish not to accept.

I crossed to the mantelpiece and looked more closely at the
model ships. Pointing to what I judged to be a mid-nine-
teenth century clipper, I said: "This is charming. Did you
make it?"

He smiled. "I'm rather pleased with that one."

"With very good reason," I said warmly. "It's beautifully
done. It must be a fascinating hobby."

Edwards emitted a little sigh. "It's rather more than a
hobby with me now, I'm afraid," he said ruefully.

"So you sell them?"

"Dear me, yes. There's quite a good market for this sort of
thing, you know—you'd be surprised. Bills must be paid, Mr.
Frazer," he went on diffidently, as if loath to bring up the
sordid question of earning a living. "Making ships seems to
be my only professional qualification."

"Well, these are certainly professional," I said.

He smiled his distant smile; then he took me by the elbow.
"Come into my den for a minute; I'll show you some of my
other pieces."

"I'd like that," I said.

"I've always been fascinated by ships," said Edwards,
when we were in his study-cum-workshop. "Naval history—
the age of sail—all that sort of thing."

"Were you in the Navy?" I inquired.

Edwards shook his head regretfully. "Alas, no," he said.
"It was always my ambition, but they turned me down—
said I had a dicky heart. Absolute nonsense, of course; I've
never had a day's illness in my life." He smiled rather pathetically. "So instead of the real thing I have to be content with
models. Come over here a minute."

He led me to the other side of the table. "Mind you," he went on, warming to his subject, "model ships have their romance too, you know. Like this one, for instance." He picked up a model of a sailing ship and handed it to me.

I fingered it for a moment and said: "It's beautiful."

"Yes," said Edwards slowly, "but I'm a little concerned about that one."

"Why?" I asked. "It looks perfect to me."

"Do you really think so?" He shook his head dubiously. "It's a funny thing, but I'm not quite sure whether she's genuine or not."

Mystified, I repeated: "Genuine?"

Edwards gave an indulgent chuckle. "I'm sorry, Mr. Frazer. Of course, this must sound like Greek to you. Let me explain. All the models I build are reconstructions of actual vessels: ships that really existed."

"You mean they're scale models," I said, impressed in spite of myself.

"Well, not exactly scale models, although I naturally try to reconstruct them as accurately as possible. I work mainly from old prints, you know. This one's a frigate called the *North Star*—he pointed to an illustration in an open book on the table—"that's it there."

"Ah, yes," I said. I looked at the illustration in the book and compared it with the model. To me the likeness seemed almost uncanny, and I told him so.

Edwards acknowledged my compliment with a shrug. He went on: "There's an interesting story attached to the *North Star*. She left Plymouth Harbour one morning in April, 1794. She was only a few miles out into the Channel when a freak storm blew up; one of the worst in history. It seemed that nothing could live in such a storm and yet, thanks to the prayers of the local people and the courage of the rescuers, nearly eighty men were saved. In that sort of storm it was a miracle and, indeed, that's how it was regarded at the time." He looked at me very directly and I noticed that, oddly enough, his eyes were no longer watery and short-sighted. "Out of the entire crew, only the captain and the first mate were lost."

I regarded Edwards with renewed interest. "That's certainly a remarkable story," I remarked. I examined the model again. "And a very beautiful model."

But Edwards shook his head. "I'm still not happy about it." He broke off and pointed to the book. "I have a nasty feeling that this illustration may not be genuine, that it's not really the *North Star*. What do you think, Mr. Frazer?"

I was conscious that he was now eyeing me keenly. I said lightly: "I'm afraid I wouldn't know, sir. I know very little about these things."

There was a light footstep outside and Anya appeared in the doorway. "Tea's ready, Uncle Donald," she told him.

"Good girl," said Edwards. He clasped my elbow. "Come along, Mr. Frazer. I've taken up quite enough of your valuable time. I do hope I haven't been boring you."

"Far from it," I said, with genuine feeling, and followed Edwards into the sitting-room . . .

2

The next morning I was making coffee when the telephone rang. A curt voice, not immediately recognisable, said: "Frazer?"

"Speaking," I said. "Who's that?"

"This is Crombie. I believe you telephoned me."

"Yes, I tried to get you last night. I've got something to tell you, Crombie."

"Is it important?"

"I think so," I said.

Crombie hesitated for a moment, then said: "Can you be at my club—the Royal Service in St James's—at twelve-thirty?"

"I'll be there," I promised.

Back in the kitchen I had drunk half my coffee when the doorbell rang. I was surprised to find that the caller was Helen.

"Hello," I said, "I thought you were Mrs. Glover. I was just going to ask you to clean out the fridge."

Helen appeared to be serene and composed. "I'd be delighted if I had a little more time, but I'm on my way to the hairdresser and I'm late already."

I looked at her hair, which to me seemed to defy improvement. "Actually, I'm in a bit of a rush myself," I said, "but we might work in a cup of coffee. I've just made some."

"Sorry, darling," said Helen. "I just looked in about the message you left last night. You want to see me about something, don't you?"

I nodded. "I was wondering if you'd do me a favour."

"If I can. What is it?"

I hesitated for a moment. "This may seem rather an odd request," I said, "but I'd like you to make out a list for me."

Helen raised her eyebrows. "A list? A list of what?"

"A list of all Harry's friends and acquaintances."

Helen looked completely mystified.

"I probably know quite a lot of them myself," I added, "but I doubt if I know all of them. Will you do it?"

"But why on earth do you want it?"

I said deliberately: "I'm trying to find Harry, that's why."

Helen laughed. "But, darling, why so dramatic? You talk as if Harry had disappeared."

"Well, hasn't he?" I said.

"Of course he hasn't," she replied indulgently. "I wouldn't mind betting that any day now we'll get a picture postcard from Monte Carlo or somewhere, saying that he's having a whale of a time—on someone else's money."

"Possibly," I said. "But supposing we don't get a postcard? I can't afford to wait. I've got to find Harry."

"But why?" she persisted. "You didn't feel like this when you got back from Henton. I thought you'd given him up as a bad job."

"Perhaps I did," I said, "but I've changed my mind."

"Why? Has anything happened?"

I shrugged. "I've thought better of it, that's all."

"Why this sudden concern for Harry?" she demanded. "I thought you were simply going to cut your losses and forget him." She came a little closer to me. "Tim, if it's the money that's worrying you—well, you know my feelings about that."

"You can put that right out of your head. You are positively not paying Harry's debts for him."

"So it is the money," she said accusingly.

"The money comes into it," I said. "Why the hell should Harry get away with it? Why should someone else always carry the can for him?"

"No reason at all," said Helen ruefully, "but he always seems to land on his feet. Are the firm's creditors making a nuisance of themselves?"

"No more than usual."

"Then why this sudden change of heart?"

"I've told you," I said.

"You haven't told me anything," broke in Helen vehemently, "except that you must find Harry. Is there another reason why you must find him, apart from the money?"

"No," I said shortly.

"Is Harry in any sort of trouble?"

I smiled. "You know Harry—he's always in some sort of trouble."

She shook her head impatiently. "You know what I mean—serious trouble."

I thought for a moment. Helen was no fool and it wouldn't help matters to try and bluff her. I temporised. "Why should he be? Besides, even if he is, he can take care of himself."

"I'm not so sure about that. Tim, as far as Harry's concerned, there's no need to hide anything from me—you know that. You'd be surprised what I've had to put up with since we've been engaged."

"Nothing would surprise me about Harry," I said dryly.

"All the same, I'm under some obligation to him," she argued. "If he's in some sort of trouble I want to know about it."

"If I knew anything, I'd tell you," I assured her. "But I'm just as much in the dark as you are."

Obviously Helen was suspicious: before I'd met Ross I had, in effect, shrugged my shoulders and dismissed Harry Denston. Now, for no apparent reason that she could see, I was as anxious to find him as she was herself.

"I've heard again from the Official Receiver," I hedged at length, "and I've got to find Harry as quickly as possible. If you can let me have that list of his friends I'll be very grateful."

"Is that all you're going to tell me?" demanded Helen.

"It's all I can tell you."

"All right," she said resignedly, and I felt a quick rush of relief. "I'll get started on the list straight away and drop it in sometime tomorrow, probably after the theatre."

I smiled, in an attempt to break the tension between us. "Thanks for your co-operation, Helen," I said.

She glanced at her watch. "I must fly. I'm late as it is." She looked at me almost appealingly and seemed about to say something. Then she changed her mind and hurried out of the flat.

3

Crombie fitted perfectly into the sedate and somewhat rarefied atmosphere of the Royal Service Club: his sober brown tweeds became him like a faultless uniform; he wore a regimental tie; his brown shoes shone like chestnuts.

We sat together in a corner of the smoking-room. The place was practically deserted except for a small group at the fender and two venerable white-moustached warriors in the opposite corner.

A waiter appeared with two glasses of sherry on a silver tray. Crombie waited until the man was out of earshot before he said: "This little girl in Cobham—you didn't by any chance find out her surname, I suppose?"

"I'm afraid not," I said. "Anya was all I heard. Edwards simply said that she was his neice and that she spent most of her time with them." I sipped my sherry and lit a cigarette. "I suppose the name Anya could be a coincidence?"

"It could be," said Crombie.

"But you don't think it is?"

"Let's take a look at the facts: Anya was the name mentioned by Anstrov, the Russian sailor who died. Right?"

"Right," I said. "The chap was delirious and half out of his mind, but I heard him say the name 'Anya' several times."

Crombie nodded. "Next thing: Anstrov had some sort of tie-up with Harry Denston and was supposed to pick up his car. Instead, *you* picked it up and found a pair of spectacles in it. The spectacles belonged to a woman called Mrs. Edwards who, curiously enough, has a niece called Anya." Crombie looked at me quizzically. "Don't you think all this is stretching the long arm of coincidence a little *too* far?"

"I suppose it is," I said, "but I can't help thinking of Donald Edwards and his wife. They're the most harmless looking couple you could possibly imagine."

Crombie smiled indulgently. "It's surprising how many apparently innocuous people turn up on the front pages of the newspapers. During the war we once picked up a German intelligence agent who acted Father Christmas in the same village for three years. However, let's just run over your description of Donald Edwards again, shall we? Just to see if there's anything you've missed."

I thought for a moment. "I should think he's about fifty-five or six," I said. "About five feet ten; white hair, getting thin on top. Seemed a trifle absent-minded—the professor type. A bit on the shabby side: old greasy flannel trousers, double-breasted blazer with brass buttons, shoes down at heel—"

"Were they regimental buttons on the blazer?" interjected Crombie.

"No, plain; I particularly noticed that. I think that's about all, except that he carried his handkerchief in his left cuff."

"Anything else you can remember about him?"

"Nothing, I'm afraid. He was very taken up with his model ships, of course. Especially one called the *North Star*."

Crombie thoughtfully looked at his sherry. "And Mrs. Edwards?"

"About the same age as her husband, and a bit taller," I said. "Dark—just beginning to go grey. Short-sighted, I should imagine. Seems to wear the trousers in the family, but one can never really tell. Obviously very fond of the little girl, Anya."

Crombie nodded non-committally, drained his glass, and beckoned to the waiter.

When fresh drinks had been brought Crombie said: "Hasn't Helen Baker any idea where Denston might be?"

"I saw her this morning," I replied. "She's got a theory that he's on the Riviera, having a holiday at someone else's expense. I must admit that's his usual form."

"He's not on the Riviera this time," said Crombie decidedly.

I leaned forward and lowered my voice. "Just why do you want Harry Denston?" I asked bluntly.

"You asked Ross that question," remarked Crombie.

"I know I did, and he didn't give me a satisfactory answer."

"I'm afraid I can't either," said Crombie composedly; "at least, not at the moment. And even if I could, I'm not sure that I would, Frazer. Believe me, in this job there are times when it's best not to know all the whys and wherefores. It's better just to do the job, avoid complications as far as possible and not get involved. In many cases, the less you know the better." Crombie sat back in his chair and regarded me almost paternally.

"That's not quite as easy as it sounds," I said with a show of impatience, "not for me, at any rate. Harry Denston and I were partners, don't forget. That's why Ross gave me the job in the first place."

"Well?"

I was finding Crombie's unconcern faintly irritating. "I must know *something* of what's going on," I said lamely.

"But you *do* know what's going on; we're trying to find Harry Denston."

"That isn't enough," I said. "I want to know why I'm looking for Harry and what's going to happen when I find him."

"One thing at a time," said Crombie placidly. "Why

should you worry about what happens to him? He's no friend of yours."

"That's where you're wrong," I protested.

"But damn it, man," said Crombie patiently, "he wrecked your business and he owes you a stack of money. Hardly a basis for a beautiful friendship."

"That's as maybe," I said. "But I know Harry better than most people and, strange as it may seem, I still have a soft spot for him."

"It seems strange enough," murmured Crombie.

"I was damned annoyed when he didn't turn up at Henton," I went on, "but I've cooled off a bit since then. He's liable to do the craziest things, yet I have to admit I can't help feeling some sympathy towards him."

"I see," said Crombie. "I know what you mean, of course. I've had friends like Harry Denston, too."

"Well, what happens now?" I demanded.

Crombie put down his glass. "There's only one thing I can tell you," he said, obviously choosing his words with care. "If you really like Harry Denston as much as you say you do"— he broke off and rapped gently on the table with his finger-tips—"then you've got to find him. You'll certainly be doing him a favour—a big favour." He got up from his chair and compared his watch with the clock over the mantelpiece. "And now you'll have to excuse me; I've got a luncheon appointment."

"There's just one thing, Crombie," I said. "What shall I do with Harry's car?"

"Have you got a car of your own?"

"Not at the moment. I had to sell it."

"Then I should go on using Harry's," said Crombie.

Back in my flat I tried to think detachedly about Harry

E

Denston: Harry, who, whatever his faults—and they were many—feared nothing on two legs or four; Harry, whose get-rich-quick schemes were the talk of a dozen clubs and cocktail bars; Harry, who always had a "red-hot one" to beat the favourite; Harry, whose charm had even overwhelmed Helen Baker. I wondered what Crombie had meant when he said I'd be doing Harry a favour by finding him.

My reverie was interrupted by the telephone. I walked over to it and lifted the receiver.

A throaty voice with a Cockney accent said: "Is that Regal 7211?"

"Yes," I said. "Who's that?"

"I just seen your advert in the paper," said the voice.

"What advert?" I demanded, slightly taken aback.

"In the *Evening Mail*, mate. The Hillman Minx. Sounds just the sorta bus I've bin looking for."

"I think you must have got the wrong number," I said. "I haven't advertised any car for sale."

"Now, wait a minute," said the voice. "That's Regal 7211, ain't it?"

"Yes."

"Well, 'ave you or 'ave you not got a 1956 drop 'ead Hillman Minx, one owner, thirty thousand on the speedo?"

"Yes," I said, "but what—"

"Well, what are you going on about then?" interrupted the voice aggressively. "Your advert's in the *Evening Mail*. Right?"

"Wrong," I corrected.

"Look, I'm a busy man, mister," said the voice in the tone of a man whose patience is sorely tried. "Get yerself sorted out an' call me back, will you? Tupper's the name, Edgar Tupper. Ring me back at Waltham Cross 965." There was a click as he slammed the receiver.

Obviously the man was referring to Harry's car: the details were correct, even to the mileage on the speedometer.

I had bought a midday edition of the *Evening Mail* on the way back from Crombie's club and I opened it at the Classified Advertisements. Near the bottom of the page I read: *Hillman Minx, 1956. Drophead. One owner. 30,000 miles. Offers. Regal 7211.*

I stared at the advertisement for a moment or two. Someone knew that I had Harry's car, and evidently wanted it badly. I made up my mind quickly, picked up the telephone, and asked the operator for Waltham Cross 965.

The same voice answered: "Tupper's Garage."

"My name's Frazer," I said. "You spoke to me a few minutes ago about that advertisement in the *Mail*."

"Ho!" said Tupper. "So you've recovered yer memory, 'ave yer?"

"Are you interested in the car?" I asked.

"Well, I wasn't phoning about your 'ealth," said Tupper with weighty sarcasm. "Bring 'er round an' let's 'ave a dekko at 'er."

"Where are you?" I asked.

"On the Cheshunt Road, a coupla miles past Waltham Cross. Tupper's Garage—you can't miss it."

"What time would suit you?"

"Any time, mate. I'm 'ere all day, and 'arf the ruddy night!"

Tupper's Garage proved to be an unimpressive establishment. In the sales yard were three cars, their prices optimistically chalked on the windscreens: a battered Baby Austin, a villainous looking MG of *circa* 1936, and a station wagon. There were two petrol pumps and behind them a small concrete and glass structure which I presumed did duty as an office.

Tupper was filling a customer's car from one of the pumps. He was a stout and disreputable individual in the late fifties. He wore deplorable trousers, Wellington boots, an ancient cardigan, and, incongruously, a battered homburg. Mr. Tupper, like his clothes, had clearly seen better days. He inspired in me an immediate feeling of mistrust.

When he had finished at the petrol pump, Tupper walked towards me, wiping his hand on the seat of his trousers. He looked at me with little friendliness in his expression.

"My name's Frazer," I explained. "You telephoned me about the Hillman. D'you want to have a look at it?"

"Might as well," nodded Tupper, and we walked over to the car together.

He shuffled round the car, examining the bodywork. Then, breathing heavily, he inserted his bulk into the driving seat and started the engine. He listened for a moment, grunting non-committally.

"Not bad," said Tupper a moment later, with his head under the bonnet, "seen worse." Then he faced me. "Wotcher want for it?"

I assumed a slightly vacuous expression. "Oh, I don't know," I replied vaguely. "What do you think?"

Tupper tilted his hat to the back of his head and regarded me with extreme disbelief. "Cor stone me! You're a right one, you are. First you forgets about your advert and now you don't know how much you want for the ruddy car!"

"Well, I hadn't given it a lot of thought," I said airily. "I only decided to sell it on the spur of the moment."

"If you ain't got a price in mind," announced Tupper, "I'll make you an offer. Five 'undred quid."

I hesitated.

"Good price for an old jalopy like that, y'know," Tupper went on. "You wouldn't get no 'igher anywhere else—take my word for it."

"Oh, I don't know," I said.

"*I* do," said Tupper with certainty. "Five 'undred nicker. What about it?"

I still hesitated. "Is that the highest?"

Tupper's eyes narrowed. "I never said that, did I? You say you 'aven't given it much thought, so I makes you an offer. Can't say fairer than that, can I? I ain't in this business for fun, y'know."

I pretended to ponder the matter deeply. "I'm sorry," I said at length, "I'm afraid five hundred doesn't interest me."

Tupper's face fell. "Oh, don't it? Well, you must 'ave some idea what you wants for it. Gimme a figure."

"You make me another offer," I suggested, smiling at him benignly.

He scratched the back of his neck thoughtfully. "All right, then—five an' three-quarters."

"How much?"

"Five seventy-five. That's top weight."

"Five seventy-five, eh?" I said "That's quite a jump."

"Well, she's in fairish nick, I s'pose," conceded Tupper graciously. "Tyres an' everything seem okay."

"Oh, they are," I agreed. I was beginning to enjoy myself.

"Is it a deal, then?"

I did some quick thinking. Someone wanted this car rather badly, I imagined, and it would be interesting to see just how far they were prepared to go. Tupper, no doubt, was only a go-between. With a feeling of mild sadism, I decided to make him sweat a bit.

I shook my head regretfully. "I think I can do better than that," I said.

"Not with Edgar Tupper, you can't," was the indifferent reply.

I sighed and turned away. "Well, I'm afraid I must be off."

But Tupper was having second thoughts and having them quickly. " 'Ere, 'ang on a minute—"

I turned round again. "Well?" I said blandly.

"Now look, mate," said Tupper, "I've offered you five an' three-quarters, an' that's a very fair price, say wot you like. What more d'you want?"

"I want a hundred pounds more," I said calmly.

Tupper's face assumed a purplish hue. "You—*what*?"

"I said I wanted a hundred pounds more. That brings it up to six hundred and seventy-five pounds."

Tupper pointed a dirty and trembling forefinger towards the Hillman. "For that? You must be up the wall, mate," he spluttered, "you're round the bloody bend! That wagon ain't never worth six 'undred an' seventy-five quid!"

"I didn't say it was," I grinned. "I said that's what I wanted for it."

He stared at me balefully. "I'll give you six 'undred."

Again I shook my head. "Sorry, Mr. Tupper."

He took a deep breath. "Look, I'll tell you what I'll do. I wanna be fair about this; I don't wanna be difficult—"

"Of course not," I murmured.

He spoke with a sudden rush of words. "I'll give you six 'undred an' twenty."

"You'll do nothing of the sort," I said firmly. "If you want the car you'll pay what I'm asking for it. You're really very lucky to be getting it so cheap, you know."

For a moment I thought I'd gone too far; Tupper appeared to be on the point of having a seizure. "But the flippin' thing ain't worth anything like six an' three-quarters!" he blustered.

"Blimey, I can get a new one for just over eight 'undred quid!"

I realised the time had now come to start probing a little. "Ah," I said meaningly, "but you don't want a new one, do you?"

Tupper's pendulous jaw stuck out. "Wot the 'ell d'yer mean?"

"I mean," I said quietly, "that, unless I'm very much mistaken, you want this particular car. Am I right?"

Tupper shuffled his feet awkwardly. "Well, I dunno about that," he said. "I certainly want one like it."

"Why?" I asked bluntly.

"Cos I got a customer waiting for it, that's why."

"Why doesn't he buy a new one?"

"Blimey, 'ow should I know why he don't buy a new one? I never asked him."

"Let's get this straight," I said. "You mean that your customer wants a 1956 Hillman drophead with thirty thousand miles on the mileometer? I suppose he didn't also specify the number of the car, did he?"

Tupper continued to fidget. "All 'e said was that it 'ad to be like this one: a drop 'ead—same colour—same year—same mileage on the clock."

"Most peculiar," I said mildly, but I now felt I might break him down at any moment. "Well, there you are. It's yours for six hundred and seventy-five."

"Bloody ridiculous!" snorted Tupper.

"I don't think so," I said. "Tell me, Mr. Tupper, who is this customer of yours?"

He looked at me almost pityingly. "Don't be daft," he said bitterly; "think I'm going to tell you that?"

"Why shouldn't you?" I asked innocently.

"And 'ave you go be'ind me back an' do a deal with him? Not much!"

"Strange though it may seem," I told him, "I wasn't thinking of that."

"Not much you weren't!" said Tupper in tones of immeasurable scorn. "Think I'm stupid or somethink?"

"Well, to prove my point," I said reasonably, "I'll tell you, what I'll do. If you tell me who this customer of yours is, you can have the car for six hundred."

Tupper considered this proposition thoughtfully. For a moment I thought he was going to agree. Then—"There's a catch somewhere," he decided.

I shook my head. "No catch."

"Must be," said Tupper. "Stands to reason."

He thought deeply for a moment. "I'll tell you what I'll do, chum," he said at last.

"That's more like it," I said encouragingly.

Suddenly Tupper was all smiles: a state of affairs, I reflected, which hardly increased his charm. His voice too was calmer, like a river after rapids. "I'll give you wot you're asking," he said. "Six 'undred an' seventy-five."

I swore mentally. At one moment it had almost looked as if Tupper was going to come out with the information that I wanted. I said: "No catch?"

"No catch," affirmed Tupper positively.

It was obviously no use my trying to pump him further at the moment. "All right," I said, "it's a deal."

The level of Tupper's shabby cardigan descended visibly and his smile broadened. "I ain't a bad bloke to do business with," he said complacently. "It's just that I bin caught a few times—you know?"

"I know," I said feelingly.

"Well, that's settled then," said Tupper. He screwed up his eyes: it looked as if he were focusing the perspective glass of reminiscence over years of shady car deals. "I'll tell you a

little story about a Jag I pushed last week," he said. "A
lovely job it was, an' all. Well, it seemed that the geezer who
wanted to flog this job was a bit windy, so—"

"Just a moment," I interrupted. "Won't your client
want to see the car before agreeing to pay my price
for it?"

"You don't need to worry about that, mate," Tupper
assured me. "My client trusts me, see? He knows what he's
getting. He knows I wouldn't lumber 'im with a load o' tripe.
You just leave 'er 'ere an' I'll make out the cheque."

"No, Mr. Tupper," I said firmly. "No cheques. Cash, if
you don't mind."

Tupper's mouth fell open. "Cash?" he said incredulously.
" 'Ere, you're a bit of an 'ard 'un, ain't yer? Yer don't think
I've got six 'undred an' seventy-five lying around 'ere in
foldin' stuff, do yer?"

"Well, in that case, I'll bring the car down tomorrow
morning," I said. "Say about eleven o'clock—that'll give
you time to get hold of the money."

"Now, just a minute," put in Tupper, " 'ow would it be if
you left the car 'ere now and I lent you my old crate for
tonight?"

"Sorry, Mr. Tupper," I said, "I'm afraid that won't do.
You get the cash here at eleven o'clock and I'll be here with
the car."

Tupper's expression was now openly hostile. "Oh, all
right," he said sullenly. "See you tomorrow."

"Have the cash ready," I warned.

Without waiting for a reply I got into the Hillman and
drove away.

About three miles from Tupper's Garage I stopped at a
telephone box. I thought that Crombie had better know

about this. Possibly Ross's peculiar organisation would swing into action as a result of my recent dealings with Edgar Tupper.

When Crombie came on the line I said: "I think I'm on to something. I've just been offered nearly seven hundred pounds for Harry's car."

"Seven hundred, eh?" said Crombie. "What's it worth?"

"About five fifty; six hundred at the outside."

"Interesting," remarked Crombie. "Who made you this offer?"

"A character called Tupper—he's got a garage out at Waltham Cross. But he's just the go-between; he's obviously buying the car for someone else."

"How d'you know he's only the go-between?" demanded Crombie.

"Because he told me so."

There was a brief pause. Then Crombie asked: "How did this man Tupper get in touch with you in the first place?"

"Someone put an advertisement in the *Evening Mail*," I replied. "It described Harry's car exactly and gave my telephone number."

"Where are you now?"

"On my way back to Town. Can we meet somewhere? I'll give you the full details then."

"All right," said Crombie. "This Tupper sounds interesting to me. I'll call at your flat in about an hour. Will you be there by then?"

I stole a quick look at my watch. "I should be if I step on it a bit. I'll give you the address—hold on a minute . . ."

"I've got the address," said Crombie. "I'll see you in an hour . . ."

I unlocked the front door of my flat and went in. Crombie

was standing facing me in the entrance hall, one hand on a small table.

He took a step towards me; I could see that all the colour had drained from his face and his mouth hung open stupidly.

"Crombie, what's the matter?" I exclaimed.

He swayed slightly. For a moment the idea came to me that he might be drunk. When at last he spoke he seemed to be forcing out every word with a fearful effort. "Frazer . . . listen . . . the *North Star* . . ."

"What about the *North Star*?" I asked.

Crombie was catching his breath with a shuddering gasp. "I . . . want . . . you . . . to . . ." His eyes glazed as he spoke and he stumbled forward into my arms. I did not need the sight of the hilt of a knife driven between his shoulder blades and the darkening patch of blood spreading over his coat to tell me that Crombie was dead . . .

For a moment, sheer, blind panic had me in its grip. I had not expected the assignment to be confined to an atmosphere of gentlemanly sleuthing, but I was hardly prepared to encounter violent death at this early stage.

I pulled myself together and hurried into the drawing-room. As I picked up the telephone, wondering whether to contact Ross or the police, some instinct prompted me to look towards the mantelpiece . . .

On it stood a model of a sailing ship . . . and with a sudden spasm in the pit of my stomach I realised I was looking at the *North Star*!

CHAPTER FIVE

I

EVENTUALLY I decided to drive round to Ross's office. I realised that what had promised to be an interesting, possibly exciting, and lucrative job had now developed into something quite different. Ross was inaccessible when I arrived, but I sent in an urgent message.

He turned round rather irritably as I burst into his office. "What is it, Frazer?" he demanded testily. "I told you to ring Crombie if anything important turned up. He can handle any immediate problems."

"Crombie's dead," I said abruptly. "He's been murdered."

Ross stared at me for a moment without speaking. Not by so much as a flicker of an eyelid did he betray any emotion. He said quietly: "What happened?"

I struggled to regain my breath. "I arranged to meet Crombie at my flat," I said. My voice sounded odd, even to myself. "When I arrived he was already there. He had a knife in his back."

"Did you inform the police?" demanded Ross immediately.

"No, I thought I'd better see you first."

Ross nodded. "You did quite right. Have you got your car here?"

"Yes."

Ross quickly rose from the desk. "Right! Tell me the rest of the story on the way . . ."

I unlocked the door of my flat and stood aside for Ross to

enter, expecting some exclamation as he saw the body, but there was none.

"He was standing just there," I began—then stopped dead and gazed about me with shocked disbelief. The body had vanished. "But I tell you, he was standing there—then he fell forward and lay *there*," I said, pointing to the floor. "Damn it, I saw him with my own eyes!"

Ross said nothing. He stooped slightly and examined the carpet.

I hurried to the mantelpiece in the drawing-room. The model of the *North Star* had also disappeared.

"Hell," I muttered, "am I going crazy? The model's gone too!"

"So I see," said Ross in a matter-of-fact tone.

"But I swear it was on the mantelpiece!" I said helplessly.

"Frazer, are you absolutely sure that Crombie was dead?"

"Quite sure." I wheeled round to face him. "I could hardly make up a thing like this! They were both here twenty minutes ago; Crombie was lying in the hall and the model was on the mantelpiece. You believe me, don't you?"

"Let's get this sorted out," said Ross evenly; he might have been suggesting a rubber of bridge. "Sit down, Frazer. You say that just after lunch you had a telephone call from this man Tupper, who wanted to buy Denston's car from you?"

"That's right. He said he'd seen it advertised in the *Evening Mail*."

Ross considered this for a moment. "Did you put the advertisement in the paper?"

"No, but someone did; I saw it myself."

"Did Tupper give any special reason for wanting the car?"

"At first, no. Later, he said it was for a customer."

Ross fingered his chin pensively. "So you saw Tupper, completed the deal, and arranged to deliver the car tomorrow morning?"

"He tried to talk me into leaving the car with him this afternoon. I wasn't having any."

"Oh, he did, did he?" said Ross. "Why didn't you leave it?"

After momentary hesitation I said: "Well, for two reasons: I wanted to get Crombie's reaction to the Tupper incident, and I wanted another opportunity to go over the car again, just in case I'd missed anything."

"How did this man Tupper strike you?" asked Ross.

"Bit of a rough diamond," I said. "The usual type of small-time car dealer on the make. But I was more surprised at the price he gave me than anything else: six hundred and seventy-five pounds was a ludicrous figure. I don't know a lot about the second-hand car trade, but even I realised that it wasn't worth anything like that. Obviously Tupper—or the people he was acting for—wanted that car in a hell of a hurry."

"What about the garage?"

"It looked genuine enough. Couple of petrol pumps, a sort of office, and a few cars for sale parked out in front—the usual sort of thing."

"I see," said Ross thoughtfully. "Well, go on. Did you telephone Crombie?"

"I rang him as soon as I got away from Tupper. I told him briefly what had happened and he said he'd meet me here as soon as I got back to Town."

"How long did it take you?" Ross asked.

"From the time I phoned Crombie? About an hour—a bit less, if anything."

Ross nodded.

"When I arrived he was standing in the hall out there"—I pointed through the open door. "At first I didn't realise anything was wrong. I went up to him and he said something like: 'Frazer . . . the *North Star* . . .' Then he fell forward into my arms and I saw the knife in his back."

"And then?"

"I had a pretty fair attack of the jitters," I said frankly. "I came in here and was going to dial 999. Then I noticed the model of the *North Star* on the mantelpiece and I decided not to ring the police, but to come to you instead."

"I see," said Ross.

"It all sounds rather improbable now," I concluded apologetically, "but I assure you—"

"Don't worry," said Ross, "I'm used to unlikely stories and this one isn't at all improbable. Crombie's body may have gone—in fact it *has* gone—but there's blood on the carpet outside. You see, Frazer, you disturbed them. They were in the flat when you got here."

" 'They'?" I queried. "Who the hell are 'they'?"

Ross ignored this question and crossed to the telephone. He dialled a number and then said crisply: "Hurst . . . This is Ross. I want you to get on to Laidman right away. Tell him that Crombie's had an accident . . . Yes, a *very* serious one . . . You understand? . . . That's all. Good night."

Ross hung up and I mixed two outsize whiskies with soda. I said: "The first time I ever saw Crombie he was ordering a double Scotch in the pub at Henton."

Ross gazed into his glass. "He was one of my best men— and a friend. You don't make many friends in this business; at least I never have. But Arthur Crombie was one of them."

I was silent, realising that anything I might say would seem woefully inadequate.

But Ross did not dwell on Crombie for long. "How does all this affect you?" he asked.

"In what way?"

The ghost of a smile played round Ross's lips. "You don't have to go on with this job if you don't want to," he said. "We only asked you to help us because you know Harry Denston well. But—well, you're not really one of us; you can drop out any time you feel like it."

"I don't feel like it," I said.

Ross raised his eyebrows. "Aren't you frightened?"

"Certainly I am," I said. "I'm as scared as hell."

Ross's smile broadened. "I'm delighted to hear it, because you're no good to me unless you're scared."

"Put your mind at rest," I said. "I'm your man." I held out a hand that still trembled slightly. Then I mixed two more drinks and said: "Of course, it might help a little if you satisfied my curiosity."

"About Harry Denston?"

"Yes."

Ross took a drink and then put his glass on the table. "Three months ago something was stolen from a house in Westminster," he said. "We believe that this"—he paused for a moment—"this—er—particular thing passed into the hands of Harry Denston and that he intended to hand it over to Anstrov. You know what happened: the plan misfired."

"Which means," I said, "that Harry's still got the thing you're looking for?"

"Well, we hope he has. It's our job to find him before he gets rid of it. Or has it taken from him."

"I suppose it's no use asking you what this thing is?" I inquired tentatively.

Ross shook his head. "No use at all, I'm afraid. I've already told you a great deal more than I should have done. Find Harry Denston and I'll tell you the rest."

"There's just one point I'd like you to clear up," I said. "Do you think Harry Denston murdered Crombie?"

"Your guess is as good as mine," said Ross non-committally. "In fact, it might even be better; you know Denston—I don't."

"I don't think he did," I said with certainty. "In fact, I'm damned sure he didn't. It looks as if Harry's up to his neck in all sorts of dirty work, but he wouldn't kill any-one."

"Well, I hope you're right," said Ross. He finished his drink. "You know, your garage friend interests me just at the moment." He picked up his hat and coat. "We'll go over that car tonight with a fine tooth comb," he announced. "If we don't find anything you can go ahead and keep the appoint-ment."

2

I set off for Tupper's Garage the next morning. The previous night two of Ross's men had been over the Hillman with devasting thoroughness. If there had been so much as a pin in that vehicle they would have found it. But there was nothing, apart from the items that I had found when I took the car from the Marble Arch Garage.

I reached Tupper's Garage promptly at eleven o'clock. As I drove in I noticed a three-ton Army lorry parked directly opposite the garage. One of its rear wheels was punctured. A young soldier, his navy blue beret pushed to the back of his head, sat on the running board smoking a cigarette.

I went into the office and found Tupper having a heated

F

discussion with an Army sergeant. Tupper acknowledged my presence with a sour nod.

The sergeant was a large man and his burly frame threatened to burst out of his battle dress. He wore a double row of campaign ribbons on his left breast.

"I dunno whether you blokes think this is a bloody regimental workshop," grumbled Tupper. "What's up now?"

The sergeant held a tyre lever in his hand. In his giant grasp it looked puny and ineffective. "Got a heavier one than this, mate?" he asked.

"Be with you in a minute," Tupper said to me, then turned to the sergeant again. "What's the matter with that one?"

The sergeant made a rasping noise with his tongue. "It's about as much use as a knife an' fork on the tyres I got."

Tupper rummaged in a tool box. "Talk about Fred Karno's army," he said bitterly. "Ain't you got any bleedin' tools of yer own? You've 'ad me jack already."

"Don't blame me, mate," said the sergeant. "I'm only on this thing for the ride." He jerked his thumb towards the lorry. "The driver they've given me's a dead loss—sits on his arse smoking fags."

"Why don't yer put yer toe round 'is backside?" suggested Tupper. "You're a sergeant, ain't yer?"

The sergeant laughed mirthlessly. "What, and have him write to his M.P.? Not much!"

Tupper handed over a set of tyre levers. "Why ain't you got a spare?" he asked.

"Because Laughing Boy out there left it at the depot," said the sergeant sourly.

Tupper wiped his nose with the back of his hand. "Cor

stone me!" he said. "You're gettin' some bright bastards nowadays, ain't yer?"

"You can say that again, mate," said the sergeant bitterly. He left the office and walked across the road towards the lorry.

"Right," said Tupper, "now we can get settled up. Got the log book?"

"Here it is," I said. "Have you got the money?"

"I've got it, mate," said Tupper. "It's all ready for yer." He looked out of the window and saw that the sergeant was coming back again. "Oh, blimey! 'Ere we go again!"

"All right if I use your phone, cock?" asked the sergeant.

"What's up this time?" demanded Tupper irritably.

"Want to make a trunk call to Paris," said the sergeant. He favoured me with a ponderous wink as he lifted the receiver.

"Soldiers!" exclaimed Tupper with disgust. "Think they know it all. Ruddy waste of the tax-payers' money, if you ask me. You goin' back to London after this, Mr. Frazer?"

"Yes," I said.

"I'll run you to the station," offered Tupper with unexpected affability.

He crossed to a ramshackle looking safe in the corner and opened it. From the telephone the sergeant's voice could be heard, raised in loud protest.

"I know all about that," he was saying testily. "This flippin' dimwit's come out with no tools, no spare—sweet Fanny Adams! . . . Yes, I know damn well we're late—"

Tupper slipped several thick wads of notes on the table in front of me. "It's all there," he said. "Six 'undred an' seventy-five smackers."

I started to count the notes.

I glanced at the sergeant out of the corner of my eye and saw that his eyes were raised despairingly to the roof. His plaintive monologue continued: "Well, what the 'ell am I supposed to do about it? . . . Yers, they *call* it a garage, but—" He broke off suddenly as he saw the money on the table. "Reckon there's some sort of racket going on here," he confided to the man at the other end. "Lolly all over the flippin' shop."

Tupper overheard this remark and shot a look of concentrated venom at the sergeant. "You mind yer own bloody business!" he rasped.

The sergeant waved two expressive fingers at Tupper, then bawled into the telephone: "Right-oh, Bert! See you later." He gave Tupper a mock salute and went out.

I finished counting the last bundle of notes. "Six hundred and seventy-five it is, Mr. Tupper," I confirmed.

"Right," said Tupper. "I'll run you to the station."

3

I took a train from Waltham Cross and was back in London by half past one. After a glass of beer and a sandwich in a pub I went back to my flat, wondering what Ross was cooking up for me next.

I was soon to know. Ross came through on the telephone at half past two. He said: "Can you come round here right away, Frazer?"

"Anything doing?" I inquired eagerly.

Ross's voice was casual. "Nothing much. I'm having a bit of a film show in my office. I think you ought to see it."

I was becoming immune to surprises now, and if Ross

wanted to have a film show in his office who was I to question it?

Ross's office was thick with cigarette smoke when I arrived. The curtains were drawn and a cinema screen had been installed on the wall opposite Ross's desk. On the desk was a film projector, and a bored looking man in overalls was threading a length of film into it. Ross stood by the desk with a heavily built man in an immaculate blue suit.

"Hello, Frazer. I'd like you to meet John Caxton," Ross said.

I thought there was something vaguely familiar about the large man. We shook hands and I said uncertainly: "Haven't we met before somewhere?"

"You saw me this morning," said Caxton laconically.

Then I recognised him as the large and truculent Army sergeant whom I had seen at Tupper's Garage that morning. Ross, I reflected, had his staff well trained: I remembered Crombie's wickedly accurate portrayal of a seedy commercial traveller; Caxton's belligerent sergeant had been no less perfect. Ross's men, in addition to their other qualifications, were apparently all experienced actors.

"We're going to show you a film," Ross explained to me, "and you'll see what happened at the garage after you left. I want you to tell me if you recognise anyone." He nodded to the projectionist. "Ready to go?"

"Ready," said the projectionist. He went to a wall switch and turned off the lights.

Fascinated, I saw Tupper's Garage on the screen. There was Tupper talking to Caxton outside the office. Tupper was clearly annoyed about something and gesticulated with his hands. Then he jerked his head in the direction of the office and Caxton went inside, leaving Tupper looking up and down the road. Presently Caxton emerged from the office, carrying a large monkey-wrench, and walked out of vision.

"This was all taken from inside the lorry, of course," Caxton told me, and I realised why it had taken so long to repair the Army lorry's puncture.

A Ford Consul came on to the screen and drew up by the petrol pumps. Tupper shook hands with the passenger as he got out of the back seat. It was obviously a private hire car; a uniformed chauffeur sat in the driver's seat.

The Consul drove away and Tupper led the man towards the Hillman Minx parked just beyond the pumps. They stood together, apparently conversing animatedly and looking at the car. Tupper's visitor, I could see, was heavily built and wearing a trilby hat and belted overcoat.

Ross's voice came out of the darkness. "This is the important bit, Frazer. Take a good look and tell us whether you've ever seen this man before."

As he spoke the film resolved itself into a close-up of the two men standing by the Hillman. I recognised the man immediately. "Good God!" I said with excitement. "That's Nikiyan —the sea captain!"

Ross spoke to the projectionist: "Right, that'll do. Put the lights on." Then he turned to me, and for the first time I detected a trace of excitement in his voice. "You're quite certain that was Captain Nikiyan?"

"Absolutely positive," I said emphatically. "There's no doubt about it; I'd know him anywhere."

"Did this man ever see Crombie?" asked Ross.

I cast my mind back to the Three Bells at Henton. "Yes," I said. "When we handed Anstrov's things over to Nikiyan, Crombie was there. I remember Nikiyan shaking hands with him."

"Why?" Ross inquired.

I shrugged. "He shook hands with everyone."

I broke the ensuing silence by asking: "Why did Nikiyan want the Hillman?"

"Presumably because it belonged to Harry Denston,"

"Yes, but why?" I persisted. "Last night your men went over that car from top to bottom; there's nothing unusual about it."

"I bet Mr. Tupper doesn't think so," interposed Caxton dryly.

"What d'you mean?" I asked.

"He paid you nearly seven hundred pounds for it, didn't he?"

"That's right," I said. "Six hundred and seventy-five, to be exact."

"And what's it worth?"

"Oh, five hundred and fifty—six hundred at the outside."

"Exactly," said Caxton with an air of quiet triumph. "And what do you think Nikiyan paid for it?"

"I don't know," I said.

"Neither do I," said Caxton a trifle grimly, "but knowing friend Tupper you can bet your bottom dollar it was well over seven hundred. A shrewd business man, old Tupper; I very much doubt if he'd have been satisfied with less than a hundred pounds profit." He turned to Ross. "There *must* be something unusual about that car, sir."

Ross shrugged. "Well, if there is, Caxton," he said, "we didn't find it. And you know Willet's methods well enough— he'd find a baby's rattle in the Sahara . . ."

4

I was just thinking about going to bed when my front door-bell rang. It was Helen Baker, who was so obviously under the weather that I poured her a drink immediately.

She subsided rather wearily into a chair. "God, what a day! We had a matinée this afternoon—one of those charity things." She drained her glass, then opened her handbag. "I've made out that list of Harry's friends for you, Tim."

"Thanks," I said. I glanced down the list which almost covered both sides of a sheet of notepaper. "I say, you've really gone to town. Everyone Harry ever knew must be here."

"Well, you said you wanted me to put down everybody I could think of. That's what I've done—even down to his char." She leaned forward and said seriously: "Tim, why did you want that list?"

I sat on the arm of the sofa. "I'm trying to find Harry. In fact, I've *got* to find him—it's more necessary than ever now."

I could see that her eyes were troubled. "Yes, but *why*? Is Harry in trouble? Are the police after him?"

"No," I said, "not the police."

"Then who is?" When I did not answer she went on persistently: "And another thing—what did you mean when you said it was more necessary than ever to find him now; why *now*?"

I looked in the direction of the hall; I was remembering how Crombie had staggered . . . stumbled forward . . . and died at my feet. I also recalled Crombie's terse dictum that in his peculiar profession it was often a good thing not to know too much. Helen naturally wanted to know everything.

"I meant exactly what I said," I answered at length. "Someone else—not the police—was looking for Harry. He was murdered."

Helen looked shocked. "But I don't understand! Do the police know about this—this murder?"

"Yes, they know about it."

"Tim," she appealed to me, "who was this person?"

"A friend of mine," I said. "He was helping me to look for Harry and someone stuck a knife in his back. It was as simple as that, Helen."

She laughed nervously. "I don't believe you. You're joking."

"I wish to God I were," I said. "It happened all right. I saw the man with a knife in his back and that was no joke, believe me."

"When did this happen?" she demanded.

"Last night."

"But it isn't in the papers."

"No," I said, "and I doubt if it will be." I moved closer to her. "Helen, please don't think I'm being difficult about this, but—" I broke off as I caught sight of a briefcase on the floor near the sofa. "Is that yours?"

"I brought it here," she said, "but it's not mine."

I looked at the briefcase more closely. "I've seen that before somewhere," I said.

"Quite possibly," she said. "It's Harry's."

"Then why did you bring it here?"

"I went down to the cottage yesterday and found it in one of the cupboards. I was rather curious about it because—"

"Here, just a minute," I interrupted. "What's all this about a cottage? I didn't know you had a cottage, Helen."

"It's in Surrey," she said, "about two miles from Alton. We've had it over six months now."

I raised my eyebrows at this. "We?"

"Harry and I. We used to go down there for the odd week-end."

"I never knew about this," I said, and then regretted the remark.

She shrugged rather helplessly. "I wanted to tell you, but Harry wouldn't hear of it. He said it was our secret retreat and he didn't want anyone to know about it."

"I shouldn't have thought I came under the heading of just anyone," I said with a hint of self-pity.

"Darling, I know," said Helen contritely. "I feel awful about it, but Harry was adamant. He was terribly secretive and corny about the whole business."

"Well, let's forget about it," I said a trifle shortly. This cottage probably explained a lot of Harry's lost working days, I thought sourly. Then I sternly relegated the misfortunes of Messrs Frazer & Denston Ltd. to the back of my mind. I pointed to the briefcase. "You say this was in one of the cupboards?"

"Yes," said Helen. "You see, after you asked me for that list I wondered if there was any other way I could help you to find Harry." She smiled rather wanly. "Strange as it may seem, I want him back myself. Anyway, I knew he'd left a few clothes and things down at the cottage, so I drove there last night."

I examined the briefcase. "Have you opened it?"

"No, I can't—it's locked. You can try if you like."

The lock seemed pretty strong, but not too strong to be forced with a screwdriver. I got one from the kitchen and started to force it. As I worked I said: "Did Harry ever take any business papers down to that cottage of yours?"

Helen produced a wry little smile. "Harry wasn't terribly fond of work anywhere, let alone in the cottage. That's why I was rather intrigued when I found the case. I'm pretty sure I've never seen it before; somehow a briefcase and Harry don't seem to mix."

"I see what you mean," I said grimly. I gave a final wrench with the screwdriver and the lock yielded. I opened the case and took out a framed picture. "Well, I'll be damned!" I said involuntarily.

"What is it?" inquired Helen curiously.

"It's a print—a lithograph."

"Well," exclaimed Helen, "this gets odder every minute! What on earth would Harry, of all people, be doing with a picture in a briefcase?"

I did not reply. I was staring unbelievingly at a picture of a ship—a frigate sailing from a harbour which might have been Portsmouth. At the bottom of the print was the inscription:

THE NORTH STAR. 1794.

CHAPTER SIX

I MOTORED down to Donald Edwards' cottage in Cobham the following afternoon. As far as cars were concerned I appeared to be an unqualified success as an under-cover operator; I had disposed of my own Consul and Harry's Hillman Minx and now had the unlimited use of a handsome Jaguar, provided by Ross. I was beginning to see what he had meant when he told me that his department had "wide powers" and "access to funds that the tax-payer knows nothing about". I grinned to myself as I took the road to Cobham: the tax collector might well have wondered how the managing director of a recently liquidated engineering concern managed to drive about the countryside in an almost brand-new Jaguar.

If Donald Edwards had been a small boy in receipt of an unexpected electric train set he could not have been more delighted than when I appeared bearing the print of the *North Star*. Like a master on the bridge of his ship he sat at his desk, holding the print almost reverently. From time to time he examined the illustration in his reference book through a large magnifying glass and compared it with the print. The model of the ship, I noticed, was standing on the desk in front of him.

He regarded me with the utmost benevolence. "I can't tell you how pleased I am about this, Mr. Frazer," he said, and his watery eyes blinked enthusiastically behind his thick spectacles. "It's taken a great weight off my mind, a *very* great weight."

"I'm very glad to hear it," I said.

His smile was almost beatific. "It confirms what I'd hoped, Mr. Frazer." He tapped the reference book. "Although the engraving is a different one the ship is certainly the same. So it would seem that the original picture *was* the *North Star* after all."

"Yes," I agreed, "it seems hardly likely that two artists would make the same mistake."

"Quite so." Edwards now compared the print with the model. "One of the things that struck me as odd in the first illustration was the angle of the bowsprit. I must say, I thought it was rather steep for a frigate of that period, but this new engraving quite confirms it."

"So I see," I said.

Mrs. Edwards came into the room with a cup of tea in each hand. "I thought you'd be needing this, Mr. Frazer," she said. "I know Donald, once he starts talking about his models—time has no meaning for him at all."

I took the proffered cup.

"What an extraordinary coincidence, your finding that print," she went on. "And so soon after talking to Donald."

"It's quite amazing," I agreed. "But it isn't mine, you know. It belongs to a man called Harry Denston."

She looked at her husband. "That name seems familiar, doesn't it, Donald?"

"Not to me, my dear," said Edwards mildly.

Mrs. Edwards turned to me. "Of course, I remember now! Surely that was the name of the gentleman you mentioned when you were here before? The man who owns the car in which you found my spectacles?"

"That's right," I said. "You have a very good memory, Mrs. Edwards."

She smiled wryly. "Someone has to have a good memory

in this house; Donald never remembers a thing if he can possibly help it. Is this Mr. Denston a friend of yours?"

"Yes," I said. "He's also a business associate."

"I see." Mrs. Edwards was clearly thirsting for more information.

"Our firm came a cropper," I went on. "Harry Denston disappeared, owing me a lot of money. I'm still trying to find him."

"Well, naturally," said Mrs. Edwards uncertainly.

"As a matter of fact, I've taken the law into my own hands," I told her. "I've just sold his car for him."

Edwards chuckled appreciatively. "Good for you!"

"I got a remarkably good price for it too," I murmured casually. "I sold it to a man called Tupper."

Neither of them reacted in any way to this information; they continued to look at me with polite interest.

"Whose car did you come down in today?" inquired Mrs. Edwards.

"Oh, that's another one," I said casually. "I bought it out of the proceeds."

Mrs. Edwards emitted a sympathetic sigh. "Well, I do hope you manage to find Mr. Denston," she said. "Of course, I know very little about business, but it must be absolutely infuriating when that sort of thing happens."

"I'll find him eventually," I said.

Edwards tapped the print on his desk with his forefinger. "Oh dear," he mused, "if this doesn't belong to you, Mr. Frazer, it makes things a little awkward."

"Oh, why?" I inquired.

Edwards hesitated, then said diffidently: "I was—er— wondering if I could borrow it for a little while. I'd like to have time to study it more closely."

"Why not?" I smiled. "After all, I've already sold Harry's

car, so I don't suppose it could do much harm to lend you one of his pictures."

"That's extraordinarily kind of you," said Edwards gratefully. "I'll take very good care of it."

"That's perfectly all right, Mr. Edwards," I assured him. I looked again at the model of the *North Star* and an idea came to me. "I'll strike a bargain with you, Mr. Edwards," I said. "I'll lend you the print if you'll sell me this model."

"Well—er—I don't know about that," said Edwards, clearly taken aback by my suggestion.

"But why not?" I persisted. "Don't you want to sell it?"

"Well—it's not that exactly, but—"

"Then what is it?" I persisted.

Edwards hesitated for a moment, then said: "Frankly, Mr. Frazer, I feel a little bit guilty about saying this after all the trouble you've been to on my account, but—well, there's an awful lot of work in these models, you know." He smiled diffidently. "They're rather expensive."

"That's all right," I assured him. "I'll pay the market price for it."

"Donald, you can't possibly accept that," broke in Mrs. Edwards adamantly. "After all, Mr. Frazer's been extremely kind to us: first, bringing my glasses back, and then coming all this way with the picture."

"Yes, of course, my dear, I realise that," said Edwards apologetically. He turned to face me. "Mr. Frazer, the market price for this model would be twenty pounds. I should be more than happy to take ten for it."

"Ten?" I said. "But that's absurd! Let me pay you at least—"

Edwards held up a hand. "No, I insist," he interrupted firmly. "I *positively* insist. Ten pounds; otherwise you can't have it."

I looked first at Edwards and then at his wife. "Well, thank you very much," I said at length. "It really is most kind of you, but it seems much too little."

"That's settled then," said Mrs. Edwards briskly. "I'll just pop it into a box for you, Mr. Frazer." She picked up the model carefully and took it out with her.

I counted out ten one-pound notes from my wallet. "This is really very good of you," I said. "But I feel I should be paying you much more."

"Nonsense, my dear fellow," said Edwards. "I'd be delighted to let you have it for nothing." He spread his hands in an expressive gesture. "But so much work has gone into it, you know, and this is almost my sole means of livelihood nowadays."

"I'm perfectly happy about it if you are," I said. "It's just what I need for my mantelpiece."

"Splendid," said Edwards. "Then we're both happy." He pushed the notes into a drawer without counting them.

"I had a model ship on my mantelpiece a little while ago," I said deliberately, "but it disappeared. That's why I need one to replace it."

I watched Edwards closely, but there was nothing more than polite wonderment in his expression. "Really?" he said. "Do you mean it was stolen?"

"Yes, I think it was."

Mrs. Edwards bustled into the room, carrying a cardboard box. "This should do," she said. "As it's not going through the post I haven't put all the usual packing in it."

"That's fine," I said. "I must be getting back to London now. You've been most kind about this. I do hope we'll meet again some time."

Ruth Edwards was all smiles. "I hope so too, Mr. Frazer."

I got into the Jaguar, placing the box on the front passen-

THE WORLD OF TIM FRAZER 97

ger seat. Anya joined Edwards and his wife at the front door
and they all waved to me as I drove away. I couldn't help
reflecting that it would be difficult to imagine a happier
and more normal family: the absent-minded, short-sighted
old man with his passion for model ships; his brisk and
efficient wife who appeared to treat him like a mischievous,
untidy small boy; and a little girl called Anya . . .

In the drawing-room of my flat I took the model of the
North Star from its box and examined it carefully. Then I
put the model on the mantelpiece and stood looking at it for
a full minute. I found myself wondering what sinister secret
was hidden in this ship; more specifically I wondered how it
could possibly concern Harry Denston. I could connect
Harry with a speedboat, a luxury liner, or a yacht, but
Harry and this sailing ship of a century and a half ago were
poles apart. Maritime research and Harry Denston just
didn't mix.

I continued to frown at the model for a moment or two
longer, then I picked up the empty cardboard box with the
intention of leaving it for Mrs. Glover who would be certain
to find a use for it. As I did so I saw an envelope lying in the
bottom; an ordinary buff-coloured envelope of the usual
depressing kind that inevitably contains a bill. I slit it open
and took out a piece of cheap notepaper.

Written in block capitals with a blue ballpoint pen was a
single sentence:

ANSTROV ISN'T DEAD.

CHAPTER SEVEN

I

Ross examined the sheet of paper with some interest, then looked up at me. "You say there's no doubt that this Russian sailor, Anstrov, died in the Three Bells at Henton?" he asked.

"No doubt at all. He was pretty far gone when I saw him the night before—he'd been in the water for several hours, don't forget. He must have died in the early hours of the next morning. The landlord's daughter found him. Then the local policeman arrived, and Captain Nikiyan came later to collect Anstrov's things. I tell you, Anstrov's the deadest man Henton will ever see."

"Well, this note must mean something," said Ross decisively, "and Mrs. Edwards must have put it there."

"I agree," I said. "No one else could have. Shall I go and talk to her about it?"

"Not at the moment," said Ross. "I'm more interested in Anstrov. Presumably a doctor put in an appearance at some time or another?"

"Yes," I said. "His name's Killick. I imagine he must have certified Anstrov's death."

"Know anything about Killick?"

"Not a lot. Seemed a very pleasant sort of chap: about fifty, brisk and cheerful—the usual type of country G.P."

"You'd better go and see him," decided Ross. "You might dig up something . . ."

I drove the two hundred miles to Henton with my brain

in a ferment of bewilderment. Travelling along the almost deserted coast road between Withernsea and Hornsea I tried to review the events of the past few days and the people who had motivated them: Harry Denston, who had disappeared without trace and was now on the wrong side of the law; Helen Baker, so unfortunately engaged to a man who, so far as I could see, could only bring her trouble and grief; Donald Edwards and his wife, whose benign good nature could not disguise certain sinister undertones; Edgar Tupper, the motor trader who inexplicably purchased a car for a ridiculous sum and had a furtive meeting with a Russian sea captain; the seaman, Anstrov, who was allegedly dead but apparently still alive; Anya, the child with the elfish charm, whose name Anstrov had muttered in delirium a few hours before he died—or did not die.

I came to the conclusion that my only course was to follow Ross's instructions and keep my wits about me. I was now back in Henton where this strange and macabre succession of incidents had had its beginning . . .

Norman Gibson greeted me with considerable enthusiasm. Over a drink in the bar he said: "Well, you've certainly brought better weather with you this time. Have you come up to meet that friend of yours?"

"No," I said, "as a matter of fact, I've come to have a word with Dr. Killick."

Gibson was non-committal but palpably curious. "Oh, really?" he said.

"I telephoned him from London. He should be here any time now."

Gibson polished a glass and examined it critically. "With all them doctors in Harley Street," he said, "I shouldn't have thought you'd have to come all this way." He looked up as Dr. Killick came into the bar. "Ah, here he is now."

Killick greeted me effusively. "Nice to see you again," he said.

"And you," I said. "Sit down and have a drink."

Killick shook his head. "A bit early for me, thank you. Now, what's this very urgent matter you wanted to see me about?" He beamed at me with the utmost cordiality.

Killick looked so placid and amiable, so much the complete picture of a kindly country doctor, that I hesitated for a moment; until I remembered something Ross had told me about some of the people who worked for him and against him. "It's not enough just to play a part," he had said, "you've got to *be* the man you're impersonating." Having seen Crombie and Caxton in action I appreciated his meaning: Crombie had become so much immersed in his guise of a seedy textiles traveller that he probably checked through his order book every night before going to bed; Caxton, as an Army sergeant, had almost certainly thought longingly of promotion to Company Sergeant-Major, and a pint of wallop in the sergeants' mess.

Feeling rather less of a fool now, I said: "I've got rather an odd question to ask you, Doctor. I hope you won't be offended by it."

"I doubt it," said Killick in high good humour. "After twenty-five years in general practice I'm past being offended by anything."

"You remember Anstrov, the Russian sailor?"

Killick looked surprised. "Very well indeed. Why?"

"It's because of Anstrov that I'm here. I told you this was going to be an odd question." I hesitated for a moment, then said bluntly: "Did Anstrov, in fact, die?"

Killick stared at me in amazement. "I beg your pardon?"

I repeated the question.

"I heard what you said, Mr. Frazer," retorted Killick a trifle coolly, "but I'm afraid I don't understand you."

"I'm simply asking you," I said, "if Anstrov was really dead."

"Of course he was dead," said Killick. He looked at me with scarcely concealed suspicion.

"There's no doubt about it?"

"None whatsoever. The wonder is that he stayed alive as long as he did. You realise you are casting a serious aspersion on my professional—"

"What happened to the body?" I interrupted.

Killick looked at me before replying. "Well, that was a little strange," he said slowly. "It must have been after you left, I suppose. That Russian captain—what was his name again?"

"Nikiyan," I supplied.

"Well, Nikiyan came here at the head of a deputation of his men, and they insisted that Anstrov should be buried at sea."

"And was he?" I asked.

Killick nodded. "Indeed he was. He was taken out to sea in a trawler and they held a burial service."

"Did any of the local people attend this service?"

He thought for a moment. "Yes; the vicar and the crew of the trawler."

I seemed to be getting nowhere, yet I had a feeling there was something terribly wrong.

Killick's normally good-humoured face was puckered in a frown. "What exactly is the point of all this? Why are you so interested in Anstrov?"

"I'm just curious," I said.

"Come, Mr. Frazer," said Killick mildly. "Haven't you made rather a long journey just out of curiosity?"

"I was passing through Henton anyway," I said casually, but very much on guard.

The doctor looked unconvinced and faintly annoyed. "I'm sorry you don't see your way clear to explaining your curiosity a little more fully," he said stiffly. "I can assure you that I'm not in the habit of certifying a man dead when he's still alive." He gave a wintry smile. "I have a certain reputation to keep up, you know."

I was apologetic. "I didn't mean to imply—"

I was interrupted by the appearance of Gibson by my side. "You're wanted on the telephone, Mr. Frazer."

This surprised me. No one except Ross knew that I was in Henton. It might be Ross, but I doubted it. He was, I knew, no great lover of the telephone. "Who is it?" I asked.

"I didn't ask," said Gibson, "but I will." He went back to the telephone and I heard him make the inquiry. When he returned he said: "It's a Mr. Denston. Mr. Harry Denston."

"Denston?" I said incredulously.

"That's what he said."

I went to the telephone and picked up the receiver. "Hello, Harry? This is Tim."

Harry had not got what you would call a quiet voice, especially on the telephone. I at once recognised this voice as Harry's, but it sounded tense, worried, and more than a little frightened. It said jerkily: "Tim, is that you? Look here, you've got to—"

I interrupted him. "Where the hell have you been?" I demanded. "I've been looking all over the country for you. Where are you? Why didn't you turn up here last week?"

He cut in with a sudden rush of words. "You've got to stop chasing round after me! You've got to forget I exist; do you understand?"

"No, I don't understand!" I said tersely. "What d'you mean, 'forget you exist'? I'll find it a bit hard to do that. You seem to forget that you owe me a lot of money. Just in case you didn't know, the firm of Frazer & Denston has ceased to exist and my five thousand went for a Burton. What about that?"

Harry said hesitantly: "Is it the money that's worrying you?"

"Just a little," I said sarcastically. "I've got to see you, Harry—and soon. You and I have a lot of things to sort out."

"All right," said Harry at last. "I'll see you next Sunday morning."

Remembering that complete ruthlessness of purpose was the only possible way to tie Harry down to keeping an appointment I said brusquely: "Where?"

"At your flat. I'll be there at about eleven o'clock."

I knew from long experience with Harry Denston that "about eleven o'clock" could mean anything from twelve thirty to six o'clock the following evening. "Not 'about eleven o'clock'," I said sharply. "Eleven o'clock exactly."

"I'll be there," promised Harry. He sounded listless and dispirited—not at all like the Harry Denston I knew.

"Can I depend on this?"

"Yes, but listen, Tim. If you tell anyone about this—if you breathe a word about it—I shan't turn up. Do you understand?" There was a kind of desperate urgency in his voice.

There had to be a string of conditions attached to it, I thought sourly. I said: "All right, I understand."

"I'm serious," he warned.

"I hope we're both being serious," I countered coldly. "Eleven o'clock Sunday morning—and this time *be there*."

I rang off and looked thoughtfully at the telephone. I knew that it was asking too much to expect any clarification of the situation in a telephone call from Harry Denston: I remembered so many other telephone calls, invariably with the charges reversed, which had told me that "there's been a bit of a slip-up", that "error has crept in" (a favourite phrase of Harry's when something had gone catastrophically and irreparably wrong). I sighed gently and went back to Dr. Killick.

"Sorry about that interruption, Doctor," I said. "It was an old friend of mine who'd tracked me down here."

Killick smiled placatingly. "It's given me a chance to calm down a little," he said. "I must apologise for my outburst just now."

"On the contrary, your comments were more than justified," I said. "I shouldn't have asked such a ridiculous question."

Killick looked at me. "I wouldn't say ridiculous, exactly. Curious, yes."

"Won't you change your mind and have that drink?" I invited.

He looked at his watch and shook his head. "No, thank you. I've still got a couple of patients to see before my surgery: both of them, alas, ladies who can smell alcohol a mile away." He leaned back in his chair and folded his hands over his chest. "You know, I've been thinking of this idea of yours that Anstrov might not be dead. It's really quite fantastic. Whatever put such an idea into your head?"

I thought it would be preferable to show signs of letting the matter drop. In any event, the sudden reappearance of Harry, if only on the telephone, had given me more than enough to think about. I had been assigned to find Harry

Denston: the question of Anstrov's problematical death would have to wait.

"It was just a thought," I said casually. "It occurred to me one day when I was thinking about Henton and the storm and what happened here."

But Killick was not to be put off so easily. "Yes, but someone must have said something to you about Anstrov, or you must have read something about him. No one would ask a doctor a question like that without a definite reason."

"I have a reason," I told him.

"Well, it must be a very good one," said Killick. There was still a trace of stiffness in his voice as he added: "But you'd rather not tell me what it is?"

Feeling like a small boy being questioned about the disappearance of some chocolate, I replied: "I'm afraid so. For the moment, at any rate."

"Well, you've made me very curious," said Killick. He rose from his chair. "How long are you planning to stay with us this time?"

"I'm going up to Carlisle tomorrow to see some friends," I lied glibly.

"And then back to London?"

"Yes."

"I'm treating myself to a trip to London in a few days," said Killick.

"Well, drop in and see me," I suggested.

"I may take you up on that, but I expect I'll be pretty busy. I've got a lot of people to see."

"Why not join me for dinner tonight?"

"I doubt if I'll be able to manage it," said Killick regretfully. "I've got a surgery in a quarter of an hour and the 'flu season is in full swing."

I sat in the bar for a little while after Killick had gone. I thought of his reaction to my query about the possibility of Anstrov not being dead: his rather aggrieved dismissal of my theory could hardly have been more genuine. It seemed impossible that anyone but Mrs. Edwards could have put that note in the box, but what was the possible connection between Mrs. Edwards, a singularly ordinary housewife, and a young Russian sailor whose body was presumably at the bottom of the North Sea?

My thoughts went off at a sudden tangent to Harry Denston. Obviously he was not at all anxious to see me; equally obviously he had somehow got to know that I was in Henton. I cursed myself for not having the call traced and then realised that in all probability Harry had used a public call box.

I realised that I was very tired and yawned prodigiously. I had an early dinner by myself and went to bed.

2

Sunday morning was bright and sunny. I could hear Mrs. Glover busy with her vacuum cleaner as I lay back in the bath.

I got out of the bath and shaved. On my way to the bedroom I saw Mrs. Glover and said: "I'm expecting someone at eleven o'clock. Could you get everything finished by half past ten?"

She looked at me reproachfully, and in the pitying tones that women use to men when discussing household chores she said: "All right, sir. But what about the bedroom?"

"The bedroom can wait," I said.

At exactly two minutes to eleven the front doorbell rang. This, I thought, is too good to be true: not only had Harry kept an appointment but he had arrived on time. With almost a feeling of regret I realised that my assignment was almost over: I had found Harry Denston. Now it was up to Ross . . .

When I opened the door, however, I found that the visitor was Helen Baker.

She came into the drawing-room and draped her fur stole carelessly on a chair. "Hello, Tim," she said in a strangely colourless voice.

I glanced at the clock. The hour hand was practically on eleven. "I didn't expect you this morning," I said lamely.

"I know you didn't," she said composedly.

"Helen," I said hastily, "I hate to appear inhospitable, but I'm expecting someone at any minute. Could you drop round a bit later?"

She turned to face me. Her eyes had dark circles under them which told of a night with little sleep. She said rather wearily: "It's all right, Tim, I know all about it. You're expecting Harry."

"Who told you that?"

"I've seen him," she said flatly. "I saw him on Friday night. He asked me to tell you that he won't be coming this morning."

I felt a sudden surge of uncontrollable anger. "Why not?" I said sharply. "He definitely said he would."

She shrugged. "I don't know. He just told me to deliver the message to you."

I caught hold of her arm. "Where is Harry?" I asked vehemently, unable to conceal the anger in my voice.

"I don't know," she repeated in the same expressionless tone of defeat. "I can't make it out, Tim. He telephoned me on Friday and asked me to meet him at a café near Waltham Cross. I drove down there after the show."

"What sort of café?"

Helen wrinkled her nose in distaste. "A fearful dump called 'Ma's Place' or something—one of those pull-ins for lorry drivers."

"But why in a transport café, for God's sake? He can't be all that broke."

"I don't know," she said. "It certainly wasn't my idea, I assure you. I tried to persuade him to come to the flat, but he wouldn't."

"Well, go on," I said. "What happened?"

"He said he'd spoken to you and that you were livid about the money he owed you."

"I pretended to be a great deal more annoyed than I am," I said. "Principally because I was very anxious to see him as soon as possible."

"I realised that," said Helen. "Anyway, he said quite firmly that he wasn't going to see you and he told me to pay you back. He gave me the money." She opened her handbag and took out a cheque. "Here it is."

The cheque was made out to Tim Frazer and signed by Helen Baker. It was for five thousand three hundred pounds.

"But this is crazy," I said. "This is your cheque, made out to me."

"I know," said Helen. "Harry gave me the money in cash."

I scratched my head in bewilderment. "But where would Harry get five thousand pounds from?"

"I've no idea," she replied edgily. "All I can tell you is that he paid me in cash. I banked the money and made out a cheque to you. That's all there is to it."

This didn't ring true and I told her so. "Shall I tell you what I think, Helen? I think you're trying to pay Harry's debts with your own money. Well, as far as I'm concerned, forget it."

"It's not that at all, Tim," she protested. "I swear it isn't! He paid me the money in fivers. Obviously I wasn't going to carry that much money around with me, so I put it in the bank. Anyone would."

"I find all this very hard to believe," I said doubtfully.

She shrugged. "Darling, I can only tell you the truth."

I looked at the cheque again and then at Helen; the thing just didn't make sense. I said: "How could Harry raise five thousand pounds—just like that?"

"I expect he borrowed it from someone—you know, borrowing from Peter to pay Paul."

"I can't quite imagine anyone in their right senses lending Harry five thousand," I said. "Did you tell him that I particularly wanted to see him?"

"Yes, I did, but I might as well have saved my breath. He doesn't want to see you."

This hurt a little. "Why shouldn't he want to see me?"

Her reply sounded far from convincing. "It seems he's just started a new business with someone," she said, "and he doesn't want his new partners to know about your firm going bust."

This sounded a bit over the odds, even for Harry. I laughed derisively. "The whole world knew about our firm going into liquidation. We had some very good notices in the financial press."

"Well," said Helen lamely, "perhaps he feels that you'd talk about it, or interfere—or something."

"I ask you, is that likely?" I expostulated. "In spite of everything, Harry and I have always been very good friends. You know that, Helen."

At that moment the front doorbell rang, heralding the

appearance of the Sunday papers. Every Saturday, as regularly as clockwork, I went to the little shop on the corner and asked if I could have the Sunday papers a little earlier. Every Sunday they turned up a little later.

"Excuse me a second," I said to Helen, and went out into the hall, leaving the drawing-room door open behind me. The papers were on the mat. I picked them up and glanced at the headlines, and as I straightened up I saw Helen's reflection in the mirror over the mantelpiece.

She was holding a small object up to her face and at first I thought she was lighting a cigarette with my table lighter. Then I realised that it was not a lighter but a tiny Minox camera.

Hardly believing the evidence of my own eyes I watched as she pointed the camera directly at the model of the *North Star*; then she quickly replaced the camera in her handbag and moved into the centre of the room. She was in the act of lighting a cigarette as I came back.

My first impulse was to have a showdown with her there and then; to get the camera from her and find out what she was doing. But I thought better of it and said casually: "I never asked you to have a drink, Helen."

She didn't turn a hair and I began to realise why she was such a success as an actress. She smiled with all the nonchalance in the world. "Too early for me, darling. I'm afraid I must be going—some dreary people coming to lunch."

Helen's little act with the camera could wait, but I had to know about the money. I flicked the cheque with my finger. "Helen, before I accept this, do you swear that Harry really did give you the money?"

"Yes, of course I do," she said lightly. "D'you think I've got five thousand pounds to give away?"

"You had the other day," I reminded her.

She shook her head. "That's not quite the same thing. I was prepared to *lend* you the money if you were thinking of starting up in business again."

I put the cheque in my pocket. A cheque of Harry's might well be a dud, but Helen could have written one for three times this amount without doing herself much material damage.

"Very well, if Harry wants it this way," I said, "that's the end of a beautiful friendship. He's entitled to run his own life, I suppose. But what about you? Are you seeing him again?"

"I don't know," she said flatly.

"You're still engaged, aren't you? Harry wouldn't be fool enough to give *you* up."

She produced a rather wan smile. "I don't know about that, either. We certainly weren't particularly friendly when we met on Friday—not a devoted couple at all." She looked at the clock. "Tim, I must fly! Let's have lunch together one day soon—this week, if possible."

"All right," I agreed, "I'll give you a ring."

She flashed me a smile which in the ordinary way would have made me buckle at the knees. As it was, it just made me mad.

"How's the show going?" I said as we walked to the hall.

"We're coming off next week," she said. "Didn't you know?"

"No," I said. "I'm sorry about that."

She made a little grimace. "I'm not. I'll be glad of the rest."

When Helen had gone I stood gazing at the model of the *North Star*. It gave me no sort of inspiration. I found myself thinking that I should have got tough with Helen and forced the truth out of her.

By now I was in a thoroughly bad temper. I went to the drinks table and mixed myself an outsize gin and tonic . . .

CHAPTER EIGHT

THE next day I decided to make a few inquiries at "Ma's Place". Somehow I had to find out the reason for the furtive meeting between Harry and Helen at such an improbable rendezvous. If Helen had named any one of a dozen cocktail bars it might have made some sense, but for them to meet in a transport café sounded too incredible.

As I drew into the vehicle park of the café I wondered still more. "Ma's Place" was a single storey wooden hut standing just off the Waltham Cross Road. It looked ramshackle and depressing and seemed to offer little in the way of welcome to the traveller. A sign above the door told me that hot meals were available at any time of the day or night, and that the proprietor's name was Dodsworth. I parked the car and went in.

The interior was no more attractive. There were half a dozen deal tables with rough wooden benches, and on each table stood a bottle of sauce and a cheap plastic cruet set. A counter stretched the full length of the café; on it was a large tea urn and some tired looking sandwiches under glass covers. Behind the counter, reading a newspaper, sat a large and blowsy woman whom I took to be "Ma" Dodsworth.

Like her establishment Ma was rough and not over clean. Her hair was grey and straggled untidily about her head. She had three chins and a vast and pendulous bosom, and her piggy little eyes, screwed up against the smoke from her cigarette, were bright and watchful. She looked to me a pretty hard case and I found myself wondering once again what she could possibly have in common with Harry and Helen.

Ma glanced up and eased her large bulk out of her chair, then wiped her hands on her liberally stained overall and pushed a wisp of hair out of her eyes. "Yes, love?" she said.

I ordered a cup of tea and Ma busied herself at the urn. She pushed the cup towards me, with a dirty thumb in the saucer, spilling some of the contents in the process. Then she reached out a fat and mottled arm and propelled a cracked sugar bowl towards me.

I sipped the tea. It had obviously been brewing for hours. "You're very quiet today," I remarked.

"We liven up later, love," she said. "Be busy tonight, I shouldn't wonder."

I looked round to make sure the place was empty, then said tentatively: "I wonder if you could help me?"

She screwed up her eyes in a grotesque parody of coquetry. "Always happy to oblige a gentleman," she said.

"I wonder if you can remember a lady coming in here on Friday night?"

"A *lady*?" Ma vibrated with laughter. "We don't get many of them, love; leastways, not what *you'd* call a lady. Friday, you said?" She scratched her chin contemplatively. "Now I come to think of it, a lady did come in. Very high-class bit of goods she was an' all. Nice with it, mind, but very high class."

"Did she meet anyone?"

"Yes, now you come to mention it, she did. A gentleman— one of our regulars."

Surprised, I queried: "One of your regulars?"

"S'right, love. He often pops in for a cuppa and a sandwich. Surprised he ain't bin in this afternoon, s'matter o' fact."

I felt a sudden surge of excitement. "Does he live round here?"

"Dunno where he lives, dearie," replied Ma. "Never ask questions about your clientelly, that's my motto."

"Of course," I agreed. I drank some more tea and watched Ma guardedly. "You say he often drops in?"

"He was in almost every day this last week," said Ma. She leaned forward with a grunt and lifted one of the sandwich covers. "Blimey, they're about ready for someone's chickens."

"D'you think he might come in today?" I persisted.

Ma cocked a shrewd eye at me. "If you was to sit down and enjoy your cuppa in peace, you'd probably see him. This is just about his time."

"Thanks," I said. "I'll do that." I wandered over to one of the tables and picked up a fortnight-old magazine.

Ma returned to her reading. Once or twice I noticed her glance at me over the top of her paper, then she got up from her chair and disappeared into the rear regions of the café.

When she returned to the counter a few moments later I bought another cup of tea and a packet of cigarettes and sat patiently at my table. One or two customers drifted in from time to time, but there was no sign of Harry . . .

Well over an hour later a young man pushed open the door and strolled towards my table. He was slim, of medium height, and moved lithely. He wore a short white raincoat, narrow trousers, and pointed Italian shoes. I could not suppress an immediate feeling of dislike and distrust.

He sat down opposite me and said in a clipped, high-pitched voice: "You're Frazer, aren't you?"

"That's right," I said coldly. "And who are you?"

"You can call me Lester," the young man said. He seemed very sure of himself.

I said: "What can I do for you?"

Lester admired his fingernails. "In case you're interested," he said, "I'm a friend of a friend of yours."

"Oh?" I said. "And who is this friend?"

He looked me straight in the eye. "Harry Denston," he replied calmly.

"What is it you want?" I asked.

"Well, I don't know that I *want* anything in particular," he said amiably. "I'd just like to give you a piece of advice, that's all."

I lit a cigarette with studied nonchalance. "Go ahead," I said, "but I think I'd better warn you that I'm not very good at taking advice—particularly from strangers."

Lester's smile seemed permanent. "That's all right, Mr. Frazer. You don't have to take it."

"Well, let's hear this advice of yours," I said.

The smile disappeared suddenly. "We want you to stop looking for Harry Denston."

"Why?" I asked bluntly.

The smile reappeared. "Because you're making him very nervous. We don't like that."

"And who's 'we'?"

"Harry and me."

"Let's get something straight, shall we?" I said. "Is it Harry I'm making nervous, or you?"

"It's Harry," answered Lester. "You don't worry me, boy. It takes a lot to make me nervous."

"I can imagine that," I said.

Lester rose to his feet. "Well, that's the advice," he said affably. "I hope you'll take it. I know I would, if I were in your shoes."

I looked at him cautiously. "Would you now?" I said.

"I certainly would." Lester produced a comb and ran it casually through his heavily creamed hair. "After all, why be a sucker? Harry's paid you the money he owes you, so you're in clover. Why should you worry?"

"I'm not worried," I told him. "I'm just curious, that's all."

"Well, I'd stop being curious if I were you, chum. D'you know what I'd do?"

"No, you tell me."

"I'd take a nice little trip to the South of France—Monte Carlo, Nice, Juan le Pins, Cannes—the lot!"

"It's the wrong time of the year for the South of France, isn't it?" I suggested mildly.

Lester's smile broadened. "Not for you, it isn't."

"I'll think about it," I said casually.

"Well, don't think about it too long, chum," he said, starting to walk towards the door. "Cheerio!"

I stopped him. "Just a minute, Lester," I said.

He turned round. "Yes?"

"You forgot to tell me something."

"Oh, and what's that?"

"What happens if I don't go to the South of France?"

"I should have thought you'd have known the answer to that one," said Lester smoothly.

"Well, I don't."

He suddenly came close to my table and leaned across it, his face very near to mine. He said softly: "What happened to Crombie?"

CHAPTER NINE

I

I came to the conclusion that the only person who could really help me was Mrs. Edwards. It was obvious that she had written the note saying that Anstrov wasn't dead, and that there was some connection between the child Anya and the fact that the Russian sailor had muttered the name "Anya" over and over again before he died. Mrs. Edwards—Anstrov—Anya: somewhere there must be a connection between them.

I had thought that Dr. Killick would be able to throw some light on the mystery, but he had been no help whatsoever. Clearly he had thought me mad to suggest that Anstrov had not died; after all, Killick had attended the man during his last hours and had certified his death. On the face of it, Killick's feelings on the matter were perfectly understandable—no doctor would welcome the theory that he had caused someone to be buried alive.

I decided that Mrs. Edwards' message could mean only one thing: that the man who had died at Henton was not Anstrov. But this seemed equally absurd because Captain Nikiyan had identified the body.

My thoughts switched to the young man who called himself Lester. He obviously knew where Harry Denston was and had done his best to throw me off his trail. Lester knew who had killed Crombie; indeed, he might well have done so himself. Lester was working for someone who knew where Harry was and they (whoever "they" might be) were prepared to go to any lengths, including murder, to keep his

whereabouts a secret. Ross had given me the job of finding
Harry, but Harry was clearly determined not to be found.

And then there was Helen Baker; how did she fit into this
bizarre jigsaw puzzle? Was she acting out of love, mistaken
loyalty, or some more sinister motive? Why had she taken
that photograph of the *North Star* in my flat?

For a full hour I wrestled with these questions and eventually found myself back where I had started—the note from
Mrs. Edwards. I got into my car and drove in the direction
of Cobham.

Halfway down Cobham's busy High Street I groped in my
pocket for a cigarette, but found only an empty packet. I
pulled up at a confectioner's shop and bought a packet of
twenty. I was just about to drive away again when I noticed
a somewhat battered Austin Eight which had drawn up
near a greengrocer's on the opposite side of the
road. Ruth Edwards got out of the car and went into the
shop.

I crossed the High Street to the Austin, looked up and
down the street carefully, and then got into the front
passenger seat.

I looked around inside the car. On the shelf behind the
back seat was a large, stuffed ornamental tiger, and on the
back seat a square brown paper parcel, addressed and ready
for posting. Obviously a methodical woman, Mrs. Edwards
had addressed the parcel twice: once on the paper
and again on a small label tied to the string. On it was
written:

C. Bonnington, Esq.,
48 Clayton Road,
Camden Town,
London, N.W.1.

I scribbled the name and address on the back of an old envelope and replaced the parcel on the back seat. As I did so I noticed Ruth Edwards coming towards the car. Seeing me in the front seat, she stopped dead and drew in her breath sharply. I opened the door and said: "Do get in, Mrs. Edwards. I'm very anxious to talk to you."

Her attempt at nonchalance did not strike me as entirely successful. "What are you doing in my car?" she demanded.

"Waiting for you," I explained.

She looked flustered and palpably ill at ease. "Why on earth didn't you come to the cottage, Mr. Frazer? Why do we have to talk here—in my car?"

"I was on my way there; I happened to see your car and thought this would be a little less obvious," I said.

She recovered herself quickly. "What is it you want?" Her voice was perfectly normal, but I noticed that she ceaselessly moistened her lips with her tongue.

"Well, first of all, thank you for the note," I said.

"I'm afraid I don't quite understand you." Her expression was affronted and frigid.

"I was referring to the note that was with the model I bought from your husband," I explained.

She made an impatient gesture. "I haven't the remotest idea what you're talking about, Mr. Frazer."

I started to get out of the car. "I must apologise," I said. "I've obviously made a mistake. It must have been your husband who put the note in the box. I'll have a word with him about it."

I had one foot in the road, but she stopped me.

"No, wait," she said urgently; "there's no need to tell Donald about this. What exactly is it you want to know?"

"I want to know if you sent the note."

She hesitated, apparently trying to collect herself. Then, rather reluctantly, she nodded.

"Why?"

"I thought it might help you, that's all."

"Help *me*? In what way?"

She looked out of the car window and said quickly: "We really can't talk here." There was a note of desperation in her voice.

"I think we can," I said. "Do you mean that the note might help me to find Harry Denston?"

Without looking at me she said: "Perhaps."

"The note said, 'Anstrov isn't dead'," I said. "What did you mean by that? That the dead man wasn't Anstrov at all?"

She looked out of the window again. "Yes," she said distractedly. She turned to me with an appealing look. "Mr. Frazer, I'm sorry, but I just *can't* talk to you now. I'm expecting my husband at any moment, and if he sees us together he'll—"

"All right," I interrupted. "If I go now, will you meet me sometime tomorrow?"

She hesitated, her eyes darting up and down the street. Then she said: "I'll see you at the cottage at about eleven o'clock."

"I'll be there," I nodded and started to get out of the car again. Then a sudden thought struck me. "Before I go, Mrs. Edwards, do you happen to know a Dr. Killick?"

She looked quite blank. "Dr. Killick? No, I don't think so—in fact I'm sure I don't. Why d'you ask?"

"I just wondered," I said vaguely. "It really doesn't matter."

"Well, I've never heard of him," she said.

I got out of the car and closed the door. Through the

open window I said: "Till tomorrow, Mrs. Edwards."

She nodded, tight lipped. Then she drove away and I crossed the street to my own car.

2

There seemed to be everything but the kitchen stove in Bonnington's shop in Camden Town.

There were stamp albums, fishing rods, roller skates, musical instruments, ancient duelling pistols, playing cards, horse brasses, beer tankards, and gargantuan brass kettles.

I realised that going to Bonnington's was a pretty long shot, but having seen the address on the parcel in Mrs. Edwards' car I decided to follow it up. I ran my eye over the bewildering array of merchandise in the shop window. Right in front were several models of ships.

I began to see some daylight. Edwards had told me that he sold the models he made, and any of those in the shop window could have been made by him: they all exhibited the same exquisite workmanship and meticulous attention to detail. I decided that it was worth trying.

The man behind the counter came towards me. "Yes, sir?" he said. "What can I do for you?"

"I'm rather interested in the models you have in the window," I said.

"Oh, yes, sir? Any particular one that's caught your fancy?"

"I'm looking for a model of a particular ship," I said. "It's a frigate called—" I paused and then said very distinctly— "the *North Star*."

The man nodded and gave me a meaning smile. Then he opened a drawer under the counter and took out a small envelope, which he handed to me. "You're bang on time," he said. "It only arrived this morning."

I sat in my car and tore open the envelope. Inside was a small but perfectly developed photograph. Every detail of the mantelpiece in the drawing-room of my flat was faithfully reproduced: the clock, a vase of flowers, a pipe rack—and the model of the *North Star*.

As soon as I reached my flat I telephoned Helen Baker and told her I had to see her at once.

I met Helen at the front door and led her into the drawing-room.

She said casually: "All this sounds fearfully serious and dramatic, Tim. What's it all about?" She arranged herself to the best advantage in an armchair and very slightly elevated her eyebrows. "You said you'd got a surprise for me. I hope it's a nice one."

"That's for you to decide," I said uncompromisingly. I took the photograph out of my wallet and held it out to her. "It's come out rather well, hasn't it? I must congratulate you on your photography—I never knew it was one of your accomplishments."

Helen looked at the photograph and recoiled sharply. "Oh, Tim . . ." she said wretchedly.

"Cut out the drama," I said sourly. "And don't try to tell me that you didn't take that picture, because I saw you. I think I deserve some sort of explanation."

"I—I don't know what to say," she murmured helplessly.

"Well, say *something*," I snapped. "Why did you take it?"

"I don't know." Her eyes were downcast and she twisted a handkerchief in her fingers.

"I intend to find out why you took that photograph," I said grimly. "Now, let's have it."

Helen looked up; I could see that her eyes were eloquent

with misery. She said tremulously: "Harry asked me to do it. He gave me the camera and told me that—" she faltered and her voice trailed away into silence.

"Tell me the rest," I said, "and make it the truth."

She spoke with a sudden rush of words. "I just didn't think, Tim. Harry gave me the camera and asked me to take a photograph of the model on your mantelpiece. It seemed harmless enough." She clutched my arm. "Tim, I'm terribly sorry; I should have told you about it. I realise that now."

"That's very gratifying," I said. "Did Harry tell you why he wanted the photograph?"

She shook her head. "No."

"Have *you* any idea why he wanted it?"

"No, of course I haven't the slightest idea. You do believe me, Tim, don't you?"

"Frankly," I said, "I don't."

"But it's the truth!"

"Now, listen to me," I said seriously. "The people Harry's mixed up with aren't playing a game, you know. If you know anything about them—anything at all—then you'd better tell me before it's too late."

"What d'you mean—before it's too late?"

"I told you what happened to that friend of mine," I said. "I found him here, in the hall, with a knife in his back. Now, what happened when you saw Harry?"

"I've already told you."

"Tell me again."

She said, without looking at me: "He said he didn't want to see you, that he wanted you to leave him alone. He gave me the money for you and then he asked me to take the photograph. He told me to post the camera to a shop in Camden Town."

"Was the shop called Bonnington's?" I asked quickly.

She turned to face me. "Yes, that's right. How did you know about Bonnington's?"

I ignored the question. "What did Harry look like when you saw him?" I asked.

"Ghastly," replied Helen readily. "He looked ill and frightened. He wouldn't talk about anything. But he seemed absolutely sure about one thing—he wants you to leave him alone."

"Then why did he write and ask me to meet him at Henton?"

She shrugged helplessly. "I don't know."

"Did he mention Henton, or the letter?"

"No."

"Did he tell you where he'd got all that money from?"

"He told me nothing—not a damned thing." She lit a cigarette with a trembling hand.

The telephone rang. I looked at Helen, nervously puffing at her cigarette, then I picked up the receiver.

I instantly recognised the voice on the other end as that of Mrs. Edwards. She said urgently: "My husband's catching a later train tomorrow morning, so please don't get here until after one o'clock."

"I understand. Thanks for ringing." I hung up and turned to Helen.

"D'you think I could have a drink?" she asked, her voice sounding lifeless and depressed.

I mixed two whiskies and soda and handed a glass to Helen. She drank some and asked: "Tim, what is it that Harry's mixed up in? Do you know?"

"No, I don't," I said, "but I'm hoping I shall by this time tomorrow . . ."

CHAPTER TEN

I

ABOUT three miles out of Cobham I noticed two police cars and an ambulance pulled up on the side of the road. Several cars had stopped and I put my head out of the window to see what had happened. On the left side of the road a small car had overturned in the ditch.

The queue of cars slowly eased forward and a motor cycle policeman waved me on. Then the queue came to a halt again and I stuck my head out of the window once more. "Are they badly hurt?" I asked the traffic policeman.

"There's only one, sir—a woman," he told me. "Shocking mess—they're just getting her out now. I reckon she's had it."

The policeman moved on. I watched as a stretcher was taken over to the wrecked car. From where I was I could see that the near-side door of the car was smashed inwards on to the driving seat.

Near the wreck I noticed a boy of about thirteen holding a stuffed toy tiger and showing it to another boy. It immediately brought to mind a similar toy tiger I had seen recently . . .

I went up to the boy. "Where did you get that from, sonny?" I asked him.

The boy jerked his thumb towards the wreck. "It came out of the car what was smashed up." he said.

I parked my car by the side of the road and walked towards a small group of people who had gathered near the wreckage.

"Have you identified the lady yet?" I asked the policeman.

He regarded me curiously. "We haven't had a chance
yet, sir."

"I've an idea that she might be a friend of mine," I
explained. "I wonder if I could see her for a moment?"

"Come with me, sir," said the policeman.

We pushed our way through the crowd to the stretcher
beside the wrecked car. A woman was lying there, swathed in
blankets. The policeman lowered the blankets a little and
looked at me inquiringly.

Despite the blood from two cuts on her face, I recognised
the woman as Ruth Edwards . . .

"This lady's a friend of mine, Officer," I said. "I wonder if
I could go with her to the hospital?"

The policeman looked puzzled. "You weren't involved in
the accident, were you, sir?"

"No, I just happened to be passing."

The policeman indicated a man in plain clothes. "You'd
better ask the doctor, sir."

The doctor was a youngish man with startlingly red hair.
In answer to my request he said: "I don't see why you
shouldn't come along. I can't tell until I give her a thorough
examination at the hospital, but she seems pretty badly
hurt."

"D'you think she'll live?" I asked.

The doctor looked at me sharply. "I can't tell yet," he
replied shortly. He turned to one of the ambulance men.
"Come on, let's get to the hospital."

I sat on the pull-out seat at the front end of the ambulance, looking intently at Ruth Edwards, who lay quite
still with her eyes closed. The doctor was taking

instruments out of his bag which was on the other stretcher.

Suddenly Mrs. Edwards emitted a quavering sigh. Her eyes flickered open and she tried to speak.

I leaned forward. "What is it, Mrs. Edwards?" I asked.

She forced the words out, but only with fearful effort. "Helen . . . Baker . . ."

"Yes?" I said. "What about her?"

She said in a whisper that I could barely hear: "She . . . didn't . . . see . . . Denston . . ."

"She didn't see him?"

Mrs. Edwards moved her head very slowly from side to side. "No . . . she was lying . . . She didn't . . . see . . . Denston . . ."

"Where is Harry Denston?" I asked tensely.

Her expression went blank.

I leaned closer to her. "Try to tell me," I urged. "This is very important. Where—is—Harry—Denston?"

The doctor came towards me, holding a hypodermic and put a hand on my arm. "I don't think she'd better talk at the moment," he said. There was a note of gentle reproof in his voice.

But Mrs. Edwards' lips were moving again and I bent forward to catch what she said. "I . . . think . . . Helen . . . knows . . ."

Then the doctor slid the needle into her arm and she relapsed into unconsciousness.

The doctor turned to me: "She'll be unconscious for another twenty-four hours at least. Looks to me like a skull fracture."

The ambulance pulled up with a gentle jerk and I climbed out. There was no point in my going into the hospital, so I managed to hop a lift in a passing van, back to my car. Then I drove to London.

The time had come, I thought grimly, to start getting *really* tough with Helen Baker . . .

2

Later that evening, in my flat, I was surprised when I answered the doorbell to see Dr. Killick standing there, clutching a large briefcase.

"I remember your asking me to look you up when I was in London," he said with a genial smile. "I thought I'd take you up on it. I hope you don't mind me dropping in on you like this."

"Not at all," I replied. "Delighted to see you."

"I was on my way to the Royal Hospital," explained Killick. "I thought I'd kill two birds with one stone."

He took a business envelope from his inside pocket. "I was in the Three Bells at Henton yesterday, and Norman Gibson happened to mention that a letter had arrived for you from London. He was going to send it on, but as I was coming to London I thought I might as well deliver it to you in person."

"That was very kind of you, Doctor," I said.

Killick handed me the letter. I recognised the writing on the envelope as Harry's. It was only a brief note, very much to the point: *For the last time, stop chasing after me. If you know what's good for you, you'll forget I ever existed.*

I put the letter back into the envelope and looked up at Killick. "It's from that friend of mine," I told him. "Harry Denston."

"You mean the man you were supposed to meet at Henton?"

I nodded. "But I can't imagine why he wrote to me at the Three Bells; he's got my address." I put the letter in my pocket. "What brings you to the Royal Hospital, Doctor? Or is that a professional secret?"

"Not at all," said Killick. "Gareth—that's my brother-in-law—was in a motor accident earlier today. He got away with a broken leg, but I promised my sister that I'd look in and make sure that they were taking good care of him."

"Where was the accident?" I asked.

"In Baker Street, actually. Why d'you ask?"

"Well, it's just a coincidence, I suppose, but a friend of mine was involved in a car smash today."

"I'm sorry to hear that," said Killick. "Was he badly hurt?"

"It was a woman called Ruth Edwards. She's still on the danger list."

"I say, that's bad," said Killick sympathetically. "How did the accident happen?"

"I really don't know," I replied. "I travelled to the hospital with her in the ambulance. As a matter of fact, she's only a casual acquaintance. I happened to find her spectacles one day and returned them to her."

"Well," said Killick, "I hope she makes a quick recovery."

"I hope your brother-in-law does the same."

Killick smiled. "Gareth? Oh, he'll be all right—constitution like an ox. All the same, I'd better go round and see what they're doing to him, just to keep my sister happy."

He refused my offer of refreshment and said he must be going.

I accompanied him into the hall. "Well, many thanks for bringing that letter along," I said.

He smiled. "No trouble at all, my dear fellow."

When Killick had gone I read Harry's letter again, and decided that there was only one course of action.

I had to see Ross immediately.

My interview with Ross was disappointing in one way, but strangely gratifying in another. He said somewhat frostily: "I've given you a job to do, Frazer—find Harry Denston. Well, get on with it."

I felt slightly foolish.

He leaned forward and I saw that a cold little smile was playing about his lips. He said: "Are you trying to tell me the job is a bit too tough for you?"

"I didn't say that," I said, somewhat nettled. "As a matter of fact, I think I'm really getting somewhere at last."

Ross was still wearing his cold little smile. He leaned back in his chair, placed the tips of his fingers together, and said: "Where?"

I felt rather like a small boy before his headmaster. Then I saw that Ross was no longer smiling. He said: "Listen to me, Frazer. I've got a lot of experienced people working for me— people I never have to check on. I don't ask them for progress reports; as a general rule I don't want to see them until the job they are doing is satisfactorily completed. Others are younger and less experienced and I have to keep an eye on them in case they do something damned stupid." He surprised me by adding: "You're in the first category, Frazer."

I suddenly felt ridiculously elated. "I'm glad to hear it," I said.

"If you want anything from my department, then ask for it. You're strictly on your own on this job—at the moment," Ross said.

"Right. First of all, I want some information about a woman called Ma Dodsworth. She keeps a transport café on the Waltham Cross Road."

Ross scribbled a note on the pad in front of him. "D'you want to know anything particular about her?"

"I'd like to know a little about her background."

"Right," said Ross. "Anything else?"

"One more thing," I said. "Can you find out if a man was involved in a motor smash in Baker Street yesterday and taken to the Royal Hospital? The man's christian name is Gareth, but that's all I know about him."

"I'll see to it," said Ross. "When I've got this information we'll meet somewhere."

3

Soon after I returned to my flat that morning, Donald Edwards called to see me. He looked tired, worried, and dishevelled, and was carrying a large brown paper parcel.

He stood blinking at me a moment; then he said: "I've returned the picture you lent me."

I led him into the drawing-room. "You needn't have returned it just yet," I said. "You could have posted it to me later. I really wasn't in any great hurry for it."

"I didn't want it to get broken or anything," said Edwards diffidently. "I thought I'd better bring it along myself."

I took the parcel and motioned Edwards to a chair. "I was terribly sorry about your wife's accident," I said. "Have you been to the hospital this morning?"

Edwards nodded. "There's still no change, I'm afraid." He took off his spectacles and polished them on his shabby cardigan. "It was really very good of you to take all that trouble yesterday," he said.

"It was the least I could do."

Edwards passed a hand wearily over his eyes. I thought he looked very small and pathetic. "I'm worried, Mr. Frazer," he said, "very worried indeed. I've spent most of the morning at the police station. It seems that the police aren't satisfied about the accident."

"In what way?" I asked.

"They seem to have some doubt that it *was* an accident. They think that the car may have been tampered with." He avoided my glance and gazed out of the window.

"But why should they think that?"

"I really don't know," said Edwards in exasperated tones. "The police are frightfully cagey, you know; they give very little away. Of course, I've told them that the suggestion is absurd." He looked at me appealingly. "Who on earth would want to tamper with Ruth's car? The whole idea's absolutely fantastic."

"What do you think happened?" I asked.

"It's hard to say, I must admit." For a moment a jagged smile lit up his ravaged face. "Ruth was never a very good driver, you know; rather slapdash. She had a distressing habit of putting our her left indicator and then turning right. But the thing that really puzzles me is, where was she going in the car? She nearly always tells me about her appointments, but I haven't the faintest idea where she was going yesterday." He hesitated, then murmured tentatively: "She didn't say anything to you in the ambulance?"

"I'm afraid not. You see, she was only just conscious at the time. She did mutter a few words, but I'm afraid I didn't catch what they were." The lie came easily. "Possibly the doctor could help you."

"No," replied Edwards miserably, "I've already spoken to him. He says that he heard nothing."

"I'm sorry I can't be of more help," I said. "Let me get you a drink—it'll buck you up a bit."

"Er—no, thank you, Mr. Frazer. You see, I haven't had any breakfast this morning."

I had a momentary vision of Edwards peering short-sightedly and despairingly around an empty kitchen. "Well, we can soon remedy that," I suggested. "I have my limitations as a cook, but I know my way round a frying pan."

"No, really, thank you. I don't feel much like eating."

"Some coffee, then?"

"No, nothing, really . . ."

I said: "It was a strange coincidence, my turning up at the same moment."

"It was indeed," said Edwards. "As a matter of fact, when the doctor told me about it I assumed that you were on your way to see us"—he pointed to the parcel—"perhaps to collect that."

I shook my head. "Actually, I was on my way to see an old girl friend of mine in Farnham."

"Oh, I see," said Edwards absently, and rose with an effort. "Well, I must be going now. And thank you again for your great kindness."

"That's quite all right," I said. A sudden thought struck me. "Does Anya know about your wife's accident?"

"I had to tell her something, of course, but she doesn't know how serious it is."

"What does the hospital say? When I phoned they merely said that she was on the danger list."

Edwards' lower lip quivered. "Apparently the next twenty-four hours is the critical time," he informed me. "Her skull is fractured and her chest and neck are badly lacerated."

I nodded sympathetically. "If there's anything I can do,

Mr. Edwards, please don't hesitate to get in touch with me."

The weak eyes blinked. "That's very kind of you. We do appreciate all you've done—both of us."

When Edwards had gone I looked through the window of the flat. He stood forlornly in the mews, seemingly oblivious to traffic and passers-by, apparently seeing nothing at all.

As I turned away from the window the telephone rang. At the other end Ross's voice said: "I've got the information you wanted. Meet me by Cleopatra's Needle in half an hour."

Punctual to the second, a large chauffeur driven Bentley pulled up just in front of me. I got into the back seat next to Ross, who looked like any City businessman on his way to a high-level conference.

"I've got the information you need on Ma Dodsworth," he told me.

"Any previous record?" I queried, slipping into the jargon.

Ross gave a faint smile. "First of all," he said, "it seems that the lady has never been married, in spite of the Ma, although most people seem to call her that."

"She didn't strike me as being exactly maternal," I remarked.

"Apparently she's got quite a reputation," went on Ross; "particularly in her own neighbourhood."

"Good, bad, or indifferent?"

"She seems to be a bit of a mixture. A tough egg with a heart of gold, if you know what I mean."

"Like Tugboat Annie?" I suggested.

"Quite," said Ross. "Apparently she manages to keep on the right side of the law."

"What about the café? What's the business like?"

"Not good, not bad. Plenty of long distance lorry drivers use the place and she makes a living. That's all about Ma Dodsworth."

"What about that accident case at the Royal Hospital?" I prompted.

"We checked on that too." Again Ross produced his cold little smile. "A man named Gareth Humphries was admitted yesterday at four o'clock. He'd been in a car smash in Baker Street and he's got a broken leg."

Characteristically, Ross had not asked me why I wanted these diverse items of information. He merely said: "Anything else you want to know?"

I hesitated a moment, then said: "You told me that I was on my own in this job. Well, that suits me. But how far will you back me if I happen to get into trouble?"

Ross raised his eyebrows. "What sort of trouble?"

"Any sort."

"With the police, you mean?"

"Possibly."

"If you find Harry Denston for us we'll back you to the limit," replied Ross decisively.

"The limit being what?"

Ross looked at me thoughtfully. "The limit's murder," he said quietly, "but, of course, we'd like you to have a very good reason for committing it. Ideally, it should be in self-defence. Does that answer your question?"

"Yes," I said.

"What exactly have you in mind?" inquired Ross.

"Someone's been taking me for a ride," I said, "and I don't like it. With any luck, I'll find Denston for you within forty-eight hours."

Ross said nothing; his face was quite expressionless—but I

thought I could detect a glint of approval in the cold, pale blue eyes.

I got out of the car. Ross raised a hand to me and leaned forward to speak to the chauffeur. The big car drove off along the Embankment . . .

CHAPTER ELEVEN

I THOUGHT it might be a good idea to let Ma Dodsworth think that I was a police officer. The more I considered this, the better I liked it: Ma would be unlikely to talk freely to a casual frequenter of her café, but if I were to throw a scare into her with a few threatening overtones she'd probably tell me all I wanted to know.

I went to see the old man called Henry and found him immersed in files in his little office just down the corridor from Ross's office. Apparently he was quite used to such requests, for within ten minutes he had supplied me with a warrant card which told me that I was Detective-Inspector Walter Hubert Phillips of New Scotland Yard. I had the feeling that if I had asked Henry for a baby elephant he would not have evinced any particular surprise.

There were only two lorries parked outside "Ma's Place" and one of these was revving up, preparatory to moving off. I went into the café and saw that there was only one other customer, who was mopping up the remnants of his meal with a piece of bread.

I caught a glimpse of myself in the mirror and decided that I looked the part. I wore a raincoat and a trilby hat because all the plain-clothes men I had ever seen had always worn trilbies and raincoats, whether it was raining or not.

Ma, a cigarette dangling from her mouth, was washing up behind the counter. She served me without meeting my eyes, or making any comment.

I took my cup of tea to a table by the wall and picking up a three-month-old illustrated magazine idly flipped through the pages.

The other customer swallowed the rest of his tea and went up to the counter. Ma took his money and gave him the change. After he had gone I heard the remaining lorry in the car park being started up.

Ma glanced idly in my direction and poured herself a cup of tea.

"Come and have that cuppa with me, Ma," I said. "I want to talk to you."

Ma eyed me shrewdly. Then she came over to my table and put her cup on it. Easing her large bulk into the chair opposite she said offhandedly: "I haven't got time to sit an' gossip, love."

"Who said anything about gossip?" I snapped.

Ma's nostrils twitched. "Don't you talk to me like that, dear," she said balefully. "I don't like being ordered about, y'know. Who are you, anyway?"

"Come off it, Ma," I said. "You remember me, don't you?"

She looked at me through narrowed eyes. "You bin here before?"

"You know very well I've been here before," I told her. "D'you know who I am?"

Ma switched on a smile. "No, I don't, dear." The smile vanished as abruptly as it had come. "And I couldn't care less. You owe me fourpence for your cuppa."

I fumbled in my trouser pocket. "My name's Phillips," I said.

"That's nice," said Ma acidly. "Fourpence, dearie—if you've got it."

"I expect I'll manage it," I said. "The pay at Scotland

Yard isn't all that handsome, but it'll run to a cup of tea now and then."

Ma's mouth closed in a thin line. "Scotland Yard? Who d'you think you're kidding?"

"Don't you think I'm from the Yard?"

"No," she said uncompromisingly, "I don't."

I produced my warrant card. "Does that convince you?"

Ma looked at me with grudging respect. She said uneasily: "What d'you want? You ain't got nothing on me."

"I'm just making a few inquiries," I said casually. "It's nothing to do with the local police—in fact, they needn't know anything about it, unless you want them to. I think you can help me, Ma."

"How could I help you?" she demanded with a show of truculence. "I ain't never bin mixed up in anything."

"You're lucky," I told her. "Perhaps you've got an influential boy friend."

"Get on with it, love," she said more affably. "I ain't got all day, y'know, so what about getting to the point?"

"All right," I agreed, "we'll get to the point. You remember that when I was here last I asked you about a man and a woman. You said you'd seen them."

Ma regarded me suspiciously and then nodded.

"You told me they'd been here the previous Friday," I continued.

She nodded again. "That's right, love."

I took a photograph from my wallet. It was a snapshot taken by me, of Helen Baker and Harry Denston. I passed it over to Ma. "Have you seen these two people before?"

She looked at the photograph and then at me. "Never seen 'em before in me life," she announced.

"But that's the girl and the man I spoke to you about," I pointed out. "You said you'd seen them here."

"I know I did, love," replied Ma equably.

"Then why," I said with as much patience as I could muster, "did you say that you'd seen them, if it wasn't true?"

Ma's self-assurance was slipping a little. "Well, it's a bit difficult to explain," she said uncertainly.

"Someone told you to say it. Right?"

"Right," said Ma after suitable hesitation.

"Who?"

"Oh, just a pal of mine."

"And how much did this pal of yours pay you?"

Her piggy little eyes glittered dangerously. "Now, don't you start getting bloody insulting," she said with enormous menace. "I done it as a favour, see? You don't think I'd take money from a pal, do you?"

"Not you," I said. "How much?"

Ma looked at me, like a boxer sizing up an opponent. "If you must know," she said sullenly, "I made a fiver out of it and that's all." Her voice took on a wheedling note. "Honest to Gawd, five nicker—not a bob more."

"All right, I believe you," I said. "But I think you'd better tell me the whole story, don't you?"

Ma said: "Well, this bloke Tupper, him at the garage down the road—"

"Tupper?" I broke in.

"That's right. You know him?"

"We've met," I said. "Go on, Ma."

She became more verbose. "Well, I can't say that I'm surprised you know him. Mind you, old Tupper's not really a crook, even if his cars are a bit ropey. There was a bloke got a Jaguar off 'im—"

"Never mind the cars," I said. "Tell me about Tupper."

Ma shot me a reproachful look. "Well, he comes up here one day last week and he asks me if I'd like to pick up an easy fiver."

"And after careful deliberation you said 'Yes'," I murmured.

"Wot's that?" demanded Ma belligerently.

"Skip it," I said.

"He gave me a description of you," she went on, "and said you might be calling in here, making inquiries about a young woman and her boy friend. I was to tell you that they'd both been here last Friday and that the gent in question was always popping in and out—one of my regulars, as you might say." Ma paused for breath.

"Then what?"

"Then I was to get Tupper on the blower and tell him you was here. And that's all I did."

"This man, Lester," I said, "the man who came in here and spoke to me—had you ever seen him before?"

Ma shook her head emphatically. "No, dear, never clapped eyes on him. I was very surprised when he come in; I thought it'd be Tupper, seeing as how he'd arranged it all."

"Have you seen Tupper since I was here last?"

"Yes," she said. "He come in here the same afternoon. I asked him who that fancy boy was, and he said he was another car dealer. Tupper said they was trying to buy a car off you, but you wouldn't part with it."

"And you believed him?"

Ma shrugged her fat shoulders. "Well, I dunno," she said dubiously. "I thought it sounded a bit fishy. I thought the three of you might be mixed up in some monkey business—stolen cars or some such racket."

"I see," I said, looking at her searchingly.

Ma was clearly disconcerted by my questioning. "I've

told you the truth, dearie," she insisted. "I don't believe in getting the wrong side of you boys."

"Very wise of you," I said. I got up and headed for the door. "Oh, I still haven't paid for my tea."

"That's all right, love," said Ma, all smiles again. "Have it on the house . . ."

I decided to go and see Tupper next. Tupper, I imagined was the type who would talk if I made it worth his while. On the way to his garage I reviewed the information Ma Dodsworth had given me, and decided it was reliable. No doubt about it; she had been scared.

When I sounded my horn Tupper emerged and I told him to fill the Jaguar up. He eyed the car with undisguised admiration.

"Nice little job you got there," he remarked as he slammed down the cap of the petrol tank.

"Not bad, is she?" I said. "Only bought her yesterday, as a matter of fact."

"H'm," said Tupper. "What's on the clock?"

"Only done about five thousand."

"Go on?" said Tupper, with more than a hint of envy. "How much did they rush you for it?"

"Just over eleven hundred."

"Cor!" said Tupper in awestruck tones.

"Was that cheap?" I asked naïvely.

"Cheap? I should say so! Blimey, it's givin' it away."

"I bought it off a friend of mine," I explained. "Her husband's just died. As a matter of fact she had two cars there and I reckon the other one's a better bargain than this. But, then, I'm not in the car racket."

"She must be a proper mug to let that Jag go for eleven hundred," commented Tupper.

I gave him a knowing look. "If you step in quickly you might get the other one cheap."

"What's the other one?" he inquired eagerly.

"A Rover."

"Aha," Tupper beamed. "What year?"

"'58, I think. It's in beautiful condition, anyway."

Tupper looked covetously at the Jaguar. "Well, this job's certainly a snip. You know, I like the sound of that Rover."

I simulated deep thought for a moment. "Tell you what," I said presently, "you come to my place this evening and we'll nip round together and take a look at it. I'll introduce you to my friend and the rest will be up to you. How about that?"

Tupper looked pleased. "Ta very much, Mr. Frazer," he said. "I'll do that."

I handed him a card. "That's my address," I said. "Come at about eight o'clock."

"I'll be there," he assured me, pushing the card into his pocket. He waved jauntily as I drove away.

Out of deference to me and a possible client Tupper had shaved and put on a collar which was very nearly clean.

I said: "I'm damned sorry about this, Tupper. If you'd got here a bit earlier you could have had that Rover."

"You don't mean someone nipped in in front of me?" he said.

"I'm afraid so," I said sadly. "He got it for seven hundred. He was a dealer, I gather."

"Bloody dealers!" exclaimed Tupper with disgust. "'E'll make at least a couple of 'undred quid on that, the bastard!"

I poured out a generous tot of whisky and handed the glass to Tupper. Regretfully I said: "Well, that's the way it goes. Water or soda?"

He shook his head. "No need to drown the stuff, Guv." He swallowed resentfully, then muttered: "Blimey, an' to think I was so bleedin' near to makin' an easy two ton."

I refilled his glass. "Of course," I said casually, "if it's just a question of making two hundred pounds, I know how you could pocket a quick two hundred—just like that!" I snapped my fingers dramatically.

Tupper looked up from a morose contemplation of my carpet. "What's the catch?" he wanted to know.

"You've only to tell me what happened to that Hillman Minx I sold you," I said quietly.

Tupper hastily finished his whisky and put the glass on the table. "Well, thanks for the drink," he muttered. "I got to be gettin' back."

I assumed a pained expression. "Doesn't two hundred pounds interest you?"

"Too right it does," Tupper assured me. "Any easy money interests me. But I ain't talkin' about that particular car."

I looked at him carefully for a moment. I knew that he wasn't going to pass up two hundred pounds as readily as that. "I'll make you another proposition," I said at last.

Tupper looked at me guardedly. "I'm listening."

"I met a man called Lester at Ma Dodsworth's place," I said. "He came to see me in answer to a phone call that Ma made to you."

"I dunno nothin' about that," said Tupper, rather too readily. "I dunno what you're talking about, mate."

"I think you do," I corrected. "But what really interests me is that it took Lester over an hour to get to the café after Ma phoned you."

"So what?" said Tupper sullenly.

"So Lester couldn't have been waiting at the garage," I said. "Your place is only five minutes from the café."

K

"I dunno what the 'ell you're natterin' about," said Tupper.

"Don't you? Then I'll tell you. As soon as you heard from Ma Dodsworth you telephoned Lester. You rang him and it took him just over an hour to get to 'Ma's Place'."

"You're nuts!" Tupper said offensively. "I never even 'eard of anyone called Lester." He started to move towards the door.

"I'll give you two hundred pounds, Tupper, if you'll tell me the number you called," I said deliberately.

Tupper stopped dead and eyed me cautiously. "Two 'undred quid? Just for a phone number?"

"Yes," I said. "Simple, isn't it?"

"Sounds a bit too bloody simple to me," he said. "'Ave yer got the two ton 'ere?"

I crossed to the desk and unlocked a drawer. I took out a bundle of five-pound notes and casually tossed them on to the table. Tupper, apparently mesmerised, watched me.

"Let's get this straight," he said. "I give you the phone number, an' you give me two 'undred nicker. Right?"

Patiently, I repeated: "As soon as you heard from Ma Dodsworth you phoned Lester. I just want the number you called, that's all."

Tupper's eyes were glued to the pile of fivers. He fought a final battle with some misplaced loyalty and lost. In a hoarse voice he blurted out: "It was Kensington 9630."

Mercifully Tupper was far too occupied in looking at the money to glance at me, for I doubt very much if I managed to keep a poker face on receipt of this piece of information.

I pointed to the money and said: "All right, Tupper. Help yourself."

He picked up the notes, counted them deftly, and transferred them to the inside pocket of his jacket. What, I wondered, was Tupper going to do with this sudden wind-fall? I thought of dog tracks, gargantuan alcoholic sessions, shady car deals—all things obviously dear to his heart. I suddenly felt a lot better about my assignment: up to now the enemy had had it all their own way, but at least one of them was open to financial persuasion.

Tupper said tensely: "If anyone asks you, I never give you that number, see? I never even seen you tonight. You got that?"

"I've got it," I said. "I don't even know you. Now, get out of here."

Tupper looked aggrieved. "Don't be like that, Guv. I got to cover meself, see? I got a business to look after," he pleaded.

I decided that I had had about enough of Tupper. I pointed to the door. "Out," I said succinctly.

He shot me a look charged with venom and left.

When he had gone I paced up and down the room for a full minute. Then I picked up the telephone and dialled KEN 9630.

Helen Baker's voice answered. "Hello? Kensington 9630."

"Hello, Helen. Nice to hear your voice. Can you drop round to see me about six tomorrow evening?"

She said: "Of course, darling, I'd love to. Have you got some news for me?"

"Yes," I said slowly, "I've got some news for you . . ."

I hung up before she could ask if it was good news.

CHAPTER TWELVE

Ross telephoned me early the next morning to say he had some news for me.

"I've got some for you, too," I said.

I fetched my car from the garage and drove round to Smith Square.

"Things are beginning to move," said Ross, as soon as I was admitted to his office. "They've killed Tupper. I imagine he talked to you."

It is always a shock to hear of the death of a person you have seen the previous day. I gripped the arm of my chair and said: "He talked all right. How did it happen?"

"Obviously they were on to him. He must have been followed to your place last night. When he got back to his garage they were waiting for him. They put two bullets into his stomach. He died this morning."

"No witnesses?"

Ross shook his head. He seemed rather anxious to change the subject. "What's this news you've got for me?" he asked.

"Someone else is going to talk this evening," I said a trifle grimly. "Or I'm much mistaken."

"Who might that be?"

"Helen Baker. She's done quite a lot of talking already, but it's all been a pack of lies. This time, I fancy, she's going to tell the truth. I think you ought to come along."

"Right," said Ross. "What time?"

"Give me about an hour to work on her," I said. "If you

come at about seven you should catch her in the right frame of mind to put quite a lot of things straight."

"I'll be there," he promised, and dismissed me with a curt nod as he turned to a pile of papers.

Helen, relaxed and happy, sat on the settee in my drawing-room. She made, I thought, a delightful picture. She wore a dress of blue angora wool, which showed off her superb figure to perfection, with navy-blue kid court shoes, and exhibited a considerable amount of very shapely nylon-clad leg. I found myself wondering how a woman so beautiful, so poised, and so intelligent could make such an almighty fool of herself.

I poured gin and vermouth into a jug, added a lot of ice, stirred the mixture, and poured a generous portion of it into her glass.

She took a sip and made a wry face. "Darling, aren't these rather strong?"

"Of course they are," I said. "Just relax. This is in the nature of a farewell party."

"Farewell party? Who's going away?"

"I am. I'm getting out of this country."

She looked startled for a moment. "But, darling, why?"

I shrugged. "Now that I've got the money from Harry, there's really nothing to keep me here any longer."

"Well, it's all rather sad, darling," said Helen wistfully. Acting again, I thought.

I took a sip at my Martini. "If Harry wants to cut himself off from all his old friends, then that's his affair," I said unconcernedly. I took his last letter from my pocket and handed it to Helen. "Read what he says in his letter."

She read the note and passed it back to me. "That sounds pretty final, doesn't it?" she said.

"It's not exactly brimming over with bonhomie," I agreed. "But what about you? Are you included in this fond fare-well?"

"I don't know," she replied thoughtfully. "The last time I saw him I got the idea that, as far as he was concerned, I was just a suitable person to act as a go-between—a stooge. Still, he's not the only fish in the sea, I suppose."

I looked at her appreciatively and I'm bound to say she delighted the eye. "For you, I should say, the sea will always be full of fish. Unfortunately, you can't forget people like Harry Denston: you can't just brush them out of your life."

"I know," said Helen. She looked moodily into her glass for a moment.

I said: "Tell me exactly what happened when you met him."

She looked faintly embarrassed. "I've already told you all there is to know. There's nothing more."

"Yes, I know," I persisted, "but the thing that puzzles me is why Harry should have chosen a place like Ma Dods-worth's café for your meeting." Helen looked at me curiously and I nodded. "Oh, yes," I said, "I've been there. It's a real dump, isn't it? The juke box blares away all the time and you can hardly hear yourself speak."

"You know Harry," said Helen evasively; "he always did like noisy places."

"There are various degrees of noise," I said. "I should hardly have thought that 'Ma's Place' was quite up Harry's street."

Helen glanced at her jewelled wristlet watch. She said: "I think I ought to be going. Perhaps you'll tell me about this news—"

I interrupted her sharply. "You're not going yet." She looked surprised. I went on: "I've always known you were a good actress. I've only just realised what a very accomplished liar you are."

"What do you mean?" she demanded.

"Just this," I said. "In the first place, there's no juke box in Ma Dodsworth's café; there's no music of any kind. The most noise in that place comes from the clicking of Ma's false teeth and the clatter of cheap crockery." I looked her full in the eyes. "You've never been near the place, have you?"

"I don't know what you're talking about," she retorted unconvincingly.

"Oh, yes you do," I said. "Your whole story was a pack of lies. You didn't go to the café and you didn't see Harry. Well, how am I doing so far?"

"I don't like being called a liar," said Helen icily. Two angry spots of colour showed on her cheekbones.

"I may call you worse than that before I'm through," I countered. "You spun me that tale about Harry because you knew that as soon as I'd heard it I'd go straight to the café. Well, I went there and I met your charming little friend, Lester. I must say I wouldn't have thought he was quite your type. I don't know how you fit into all this, but I'm going to find out."

Helen passed a hand over her forehead. "I've got a shocking headache," she said heavily, "and you're talking a fearful lot of nonsense." She started to get to her feet.

I pushed her gently back on to the settee. "You're going to listen to me and like it. Whatever it is you're mixed up in, murder's only a small part of it."

She looked shocked. "*Murder?*"

"That's what I said. Tupper's dead; he was shot in the stomach. He died this morning."

"But I don't know anyone called Tupper," said

Helen dazedly. "I don't know what you're talking about."

"Oh, yes, you do," I contradicted, "and it's not the only thing you know. You've been taking me for a ride long enough. You know where Harry is, and you're going to tell me." I leaned forward and gripped her arm; it was not a gentle grip. "I want the truth," I said, "and I'm going to get it."

"Please," she protested weakly, "you're hurting my arm."

"Where's Harry?"

She said helplessly: "I don't know where he is." I knew that she was still lying. "I'm not feeling at all well," she said miserably. "I'm going home now."

"I'm afraid you can't." I looked at my watch. "I've got someone coming to see me at seven o'clock. He wants to see you too."

"Who is this person?" Helen asked.

"A friend of mine."

"Is he a policeman?"

"No, not a policeman," I said.

Ross lit a cigarette and looked at Helen thoughtfully. His manner was quiet and persuasive. "Miss Baker," he said, "I understand that this man Lester came to see you about a fortnight ago. Is that correct?"

"About a fortnight ago," she said. "I'm not absolutely sure of the exact date."

Ross inclined his head. "Go on, please."

"He called on me at the theatre," continued Helen. "I'd never seen him before and I wondered what he wanted."

"Exactly what did he want?"

Although Ross was quiet and considerate I could see something of his underlying ruthlessness. Helen, I decided, would tell the whole tale now and be glad to do so.

"He told me that my fiancé, Harry Denston, was in serious trouble. He said that Harry had stolen something and stood a good chance of being arrested."

"Did he tell you what your fiancé had stolen?" asked Ross.

She shook her head. "He was terribly vague about the whole thing. In any case, it sounded absolute nonsense to me and I didn't believe a word of it."

"What finally convinced you that he was telling the truth?"

"A telephone call from Harry." She paused, then went on: "Lester said he'd arrange for Harry to speak to me. He called at my flat the next day and while he was there Harry came through on the telephone. He sounded absolutely desperate. He said that if he was to come out of this alive I must do everything that Lester said."

Ross sat looking at Helen, his face devoid of expression.

Helen leaned forward. "Well, what was I to do? Rightly or wrongly, I'm in love with Harry Denston and I still want to marry him. I don't care what you think of me, but—well, I was prepared to do anything to save him." She glared with a kind of nervous defiance at Ross and then at me.

"Are you quite sure it was Harry who rang you up?" I asked.

"I'm positive," she said emphatically. "It was during the call that Harry let slip that he was at Henton. I'm pretty sure he didn't mean to, and Lester got absolutely livid: he said that if I told anyone where Harry was they'd hand him straight over to the police."

"What did Lester want you to do?" I asked.

"I was to persuade you to get off Harry's trail," said Helen. "Lester said that he and his friends were trying to get Harry out of the country. The first thing I'd got to do was to pay his debts for him."

"I see," I said. "So it was your money all the time."

She nodded. "I had to do it that way. The idea was that once you had the money you'd stop bothering about Harry. Anyway, I agreed to do this, and I did it." She gave me a wan smile. "You know all about that."

"So far, so good," remarked Ross. "What else happened?"

"I was to tell Tim that I'd met Harry at Ma Dodsworth's place," went on Helen. "Of course, I'd never been to the dump—that's where I slipped up. Lester hoped that Tim wouldn't go there; in which case he'd know for certain that he'd given up looking for Harry."

"But I *did* go," I explained to Ross, "and received a nice friendly warning from friend Lester. He told me that if I didn't lay off I was going to be in trouble. He meant it, too."

"Lester seems to be a bright boy," observed Ross, and turned to Helen. "Is he the only contact you've had with these people?"

"Yes," she said. "I've seen no one else at all."

"And you've heard no suggestions as to who they might be?"

"None at all, I'm afraid." She assumed a contrite expression. "I suppose I've been an awful nuisance to everybody but—well, I was simply doing what seemed to be the only possible thing to help Harry. You see, I know him so well: he's just the sort of person who'd get mixed up in a business like this and then be made the scapegoat."

I thought cynically that this was a singularly charitable viewpoint to take, but I wasn't engaged to Harry. I said: "Do you know just how he did get mixed up in it?"

Helen hesitated. "Well, by stealing this . . . thing—whatever it is."

"And what about the model on my mantelpiece?" I

asked. "You told me it was Harry who asked you to take the photograph. Was that true?"

"No, it wasn't. It was Lester. But I couldn't tell you that without revealing the whole story."

"It would have been better if you had," I commented.

Ross pensively massaged his chin. "You mean," he said slowly, "that he simply told you to take a photograph of the model and send the camera to the shop in Camden Town?"

"Yes," said Helen. "To Bonnington's."

"Why?" asked Ross.

"I honestly don't know," said Helen; she sounded weary and dispirited. "I know my story sounds very unlikely, and I know I've been stupid."

"You've been very stupid indeed," said Ross uncompromisingly. "Nevertheless, I believe you."

Helen shot me a reproachful look. "Well, that's something, anyway."

"I only wish you'd told us all this a little earlier," I said.

"I realise that now," she said. "But I was scared stiff of Lester, and I just didn't dare to think what might happen to Harry if I told anyone."

Ross nodded understandingly. "I appreciate that you were in a very difficult position, Miss Baker. But you should have confided in Mr. Frazer."

"I know that," said Helen, "but I didn't know what Tim was up to, or who he was working for." She produced a wry little smile. "I still don't, if it comes to that."

Ross smiled gently and lit another cigarette. He said: "I understand your show comes off at the end of the week, Miss Baker?"

Helen nodded.

"Do you think you could get away before then? I'd like you to be out of the way for the next two or three days.

Could you leave the show right away? Perhaps you could fly over to Paris?"

Helen thought for a moment. "It wouldn't be easy," she said dubiously.

"Why not?" asked Ross directly. "Haven't you got an understudy?"

"Yes, but—"

"Give the poor girl a chance," advised Ross crisply. "She's probably been longing for something like this to happen."

Helen stared at Ross. "Are you serious about this?"

"Very serious. If something goes wrong during the next few days—and it could very easily—Lester might take it into his head to drop in on you. I shouldn't like that to happen, Miss Baker; I don't think you would, either."

Helen went pale under her make-up. "But what about Harry?" she said.

"This may sound a little brutal," answered Ross, "but I think you've given sufficient thought to your fiancé, for the time being. I can assure you that you won't be helping him by staying here."

"You leave Harry to me," I said. "I'll look after him."

"All right," said Helen. "Paris it is. I'll be at the Meurice if you want me."

She held out a hand to Ross, who shook it gravely. Then she picked up her fur stole and left the flat as casually as if she were leaving her agent's office.

When Helen had gone I turned to Ross. "Well, what do you make of it?"

"She's telling the truth now," said Ross decidedly. "It's a pity she didn't before."

I nodded in agreement. Then I said: "Ross, is it true that Harry stole something?"

Ross nodded sombrely. "Yes, he did." He sat on the arm

of the settee. "Have you ever heard of a man called John Sinclair White?"

I thought for a moment. "The name seems familiar."

"He's very well known in his own rather specialised field," went on Ross. "He's a metallurgist. He's been working for years on a new alloy. It became rather a joke in scientific circles, but at last he's perfected it."

"What's so special about this alloy?" I asked.

"It's light," explained Ross, "and cheap to manufacture. It's almost as strong as steel and, most important of all, it's resistant to radio-activity."

"To what extent?"

"I can only describe it in layman's language; I won't wrap it up in a lot of scientific terms, even if I could. Apparently, a quarter-inch thickness of this metal is equal to an *eighteen*-inch thickness of lead."

"But that's fantastic!" I exclaimed.

"Quite," said Ross. "So fantastic that a great many people, not all of them responsible people, became very interested in it."

"But how does Harry Denston fit into all this?"

"I'm coming to that," said Ross. "Denston got to know White and tried to borrow money from him. White refused and they had a blazing row about it. That, apparently, was the end of the matter."

"Not if I know Harry," I interposed dryly.

"Exactly. Anyway, a certain gentleman—let's call him 'X' for the moment—scraped up an acquaintance with Harry and offered him a substantial sum of money for a microfilm of White's formula."

"I'm beginning to understand," I said. "This 'X' character traded on the fact that Harry knew White and was still angry with him."

"Precisely. The idea appealed to Harry and he decided to have a shot at it. Well, he was lucky: he got the film, but having got it he decided—"

"—that 'X' hadn't offered him enough for it," I interrupted, "and he was going to sell it in the open market."

Ross smiled. "You obviously know your friend. That's exactly what did happen. However, to keep 'X' happy Harry prepared a *second* film with a dud formula on it, and gave it to him."

"I see," I said. "Go on."

"Harry knew that 'X' had been in touch with a group of East German officials," continued Ross, "and also that he had contacted an armaments combine in *Western* Germany. He was, in fact, playing one off against the other. Harry decided to do the same. The Eastern Germans ordered Harry to meet Anstrov, their representative, at Henton. They told Harry that Anstrov would pay the price he wanted and collect the film, but Harry wasn't taking any chances." Ross paused and contemplated the toe of his right shoe. Presently he went on: "First of all, Harry let it be known that his reason for going to Henton was to meet you—this was in case 'X' became suspicious—and secondly, he made up his mind *not* to take the film to Henton. Well, you know what happened."

"I *don't* know what happened," I corrected.

Ross waved aside my interruption. "Harry went to Henton. He arrived the day before you did and stayed at the pub under the name of Hemingway. Suddenly Mr. Hemingway disappeared"—Ross snapped his fingers—"just like that."

"You mean he was kidnapped?"

"Yes."

"By whom?"

Ross shrugged. "What's your guess, Frazer?"

I thought for a moment. "It seems fairly obvious that he must have been grabbed by either of the German groups or by 'X', who had found out that he was being double-crossed."

"That's how it strikes me, too," said Ross. "Anyway, whoever it is, it's quite obvious that they haven't made him talk yet. He's still holding out."

"Yes," I said, "Harry would."

Ross looked at me shrewdly. "I'm glad to hear you say that," he said quietly.

"You mustn't underrate Harry," I said. "He's an irresponsible devil, and you couldn't trust him a yard with a bearer bond or your wife. But he's got plenty of guts."

"He's going to need them," said Ross.

"What happens now?" I asked.

"It's all yours now," he said smoothly. "Get up to Henton and find Denston. Don't worry, I won't leave you in the lurch. There'll be some of my people there too. This business is coming to a climax and we can't afford to let up for an instant. You keep after Denston; my people will be right behind you."

CHAPTER THIRTEEN

The Jaguar made short work of the journey to Henton and half past seven on the following evening found me parking the car in the garage of the Three Bells.

I walked into the bar. Trade was brisk and among the customers I noticed P.C. Muir in civilian clothes. Norman Gibson and Madge were busily drawing pints and lifting the caps off bottles.

Madge spotted me and came towards me. "Hello, Mr. Frazer," she said. "We got your telegram. It's a nice surprise, seeing you again so soon."

I looked round the crowded bar. "It's nice to be back," I said.

Gibson, all smiles, bustled up. "You're in your old room," he said. "I'll get young Bill to take your bag up."

"That's fine," I said. "I'll have a whisky and soda, Madge."

Madge pushed a glass across the bar, and as I squirted in the soda I listened to the buzz of conversation. It was being monopolised by a small, middle-aged, tough looking fisherman who stood with his back to the fire-place.

I said to Madge: "This chap can spin a tale!"

"That's Will Truman," she said. "He's getting properly wound up. Never stops talking except to pour beer down his throat."

Will Truman drank deeply and his audience waited silently for the chronicle to continue.

"We goes aboard this cabin cruiser and Owd Rembrandt pushes his great 'airy face into mine," went on Truman, "and 'e says: 'If y'don't get off my boat, I'll damn well string you up!' "

"Get on with you, Will!" said another fisherman. "Reminds me o' the time old Ben Pettifer—"

"I 'aven't finished yet," broke in the aggrieved Will Truman.

"And you won't afore closing time!" chimed in an anonymous voice from the corner.

But Truman was not to be silenced. "He'd got a-hold on me," he went on, "and 'e was breathing all over me. Smelt like a ruddy brewery! Then the Skipper comes up and taps 'im on the shoulder and says: 'You can't treat one o' my men like that!' Know what Owd Rembrandt does then?"

"Slung you in the drink," suggested the voice from the corner.

Truman ignored the interruption. "He comes up to the Skipper, very slow like, and he grabs 'old on 'im. 'One more squeak out of you,' he says, 'an' I'll pitch you both in the hog-wash!' "

There was a roar of laughter. But an elderly fisherman standing at Truman's elbow nodded. "He would, too," he said. "There's always a row coming from that boat. I always let well alone—pretends I don't 'ear nowt."

"Best thing you can do, Fred," said Will Truman. "An' that's what I'll do in future; these artist blokes are all the bloody same—daft as brushes."

P.C. Muir said pontifically: "I hear he sells a lot of his pictures in London."

"He won't sell none round here," said Truman in tones of bitterest contempt. "Folks got more sense."

L

Muir spotted me in the bar and walked across. "How are you, Mr. Frazer?" he inquired genially.

"Fine, thanks," I said. "Sounds as though you've been having a bit more excitement round here."

Muir jerked his thumb towards Truman. "You mean old Will? No, nothing special, though there's always something going on with that artist bloke. He's as mad as a hatter and drunk as often as not."

"What's this artist's name?" I asked.

"His real name's Walters. But all the blokes round here call him Rembrandt. After the painter, see?"

A germ of an idea was taking shape at the back of my mind. "Does he ever come ashore?"

"Once in a while," said Muir. "He comes to collect some grub and booze. But he never gives me much trouble—does most of his drinking out to sea."

P.C. Muir said good night to me and to Gibson and sauntered out. As I put my glass on the bar I looked towards the staircase.

Walking down the stairs, carrying a suitcase, was Donald Edwards . . .

Edwards focused his short-sighted eyes on me and said: "Well, this is a surprise! What on earth brings you to this part of the world?"

"I often come here," I explained, "especially when I'm in search of peace and quiet. I don't always find it, I'm afraid."

"But this is quite extraordinary," said Edwards. "When did you arrive?"

"About twenty minutes ago."

"Oh dear," said Edwards regretfully, "and I'm just leaving. What a pity."

The boy called Bill appeared and picked up Edwards' suitcase. "I'll see if the taxi's here, Mr. Edwards," he said, and disappeared through the front door.

"Have you been here long?" I asked Edwards.

"I arrived last night," he replied. "I had a telephone message from a customer of mine who lives here; he's bought himself a yacht and he wants me to make a model of it. I told him I could quite easily do it from a photograph, but he insisted on my coming here—so stupid really, and a complete waste of time."

"Have you been here before?" I asked.

"Once, a very long time ago. It's a pleasant enough part of the country, but a little too—er—rugged for my liking."

"How's Mrs. Edwards?" I inquired.

"Quite a lot better, thank goodness. The hospital seems quite pleased with her."

"That's good news," I said. "Give her my best wishes when you next see her."

"I will indeed," said Edwards. He glanced at the clock on the wall. "I must get a move on or I'll miss my train."

It was some time later when I wandered back to the bar, now almost deserted, and said to Madge: "Could I have a word with you and your father?"

"Yes, of course," she said. She called down the length of the bar: "Dad!"

Gibson looked over his shoulder. "Hello?"

"Could you come over a minute?"

Gibson and Madge leaned over the bar together.

I said: "You remember the first time I was here I was due to meet a friend of mine called Harry Denston?"

Gibson nodded. "Aye, that's right. He never turned up."

"I thought you were going to meet him in London," put in Madge.

"So I was," I said, "but he never showed up in London either." I fumbled in the inside pocket of my jacket. "I've got some photographs of Harry Denston here, and I'd like you and Madge to have a look at them."

I spread several photographs on the bar: one was a head and shoulders portrait; the others were snapshots.

Madge picked up the studio photograph. "But this is Mr. Hemingway!" she exclaimed dramatically.

"So it is," corroborated Gibson.

"Tell me about this Mr. Hemingway, Norman," I said quickly.

Gibson scratched his head thoughtfully. "'Twould be about the time of the big storm," he said. He pointed to one of the photographs. "This fellow Hemingway booked in here. He said he'd be staying a few days."

"He didn't, though," supplied Madge.

"He certainly didn't," said Gibson. "Booked in on a Friday, I think it was. Next morning he'd gone. He went up to his room on the Friday night and that was the last we ever saw of him. His bed wasn't slept in nor nothing. Strangest blooming caper I've come across in a long time."

"At first we thought he'd done a flit," explained Madge, "so as to get out of paying his bill. But next day we got a letter saying he'd had to leave sudden like. He enclosed a five-pound note."

"Very generous of him it was, too," said Gibson, "seeing as how bed an' breakfast is only seventeen-and-six and he didn't have either."

"I suppose you wouldn't still have the letter?" I said.

"Reckon we have," said Madge. "I put it in that box under the counter."

"Have a look, there's a love," said Gibson.

Madge hurried to the other end of the bar.

I said: "Have you seen this Mr. Hemingway since?"

"Not a sign of him," said Gibson. "You say it's your friend Denston, do you?"

I indicated one of the photographs. "Well, that's certainly Harry Denston. There's no doubt about that."

"It's Mr. Hemingway too," said Gibson, "so it must be the same bloke. Funny sort of turn-up, isn't it?"

Madge came back flourishing a piece of paper. "Here we are," she announced triumphantly. "Knew I'd kept it somewhere."

It was typical of the hasty scrawls that represented Harry's efforts at correspondence.

Sorry, had to leave in a hurry. Bit of urgent business cropped up. J. Hemingway.

I was just putting the letter in my pocket when Dr. Killick poked his head round the door. Seeing me, he came into the bar. "Well, well," he said expansively, "good evening to you, Mr. Frazer. What brings you to this part of the world?" He sat down and gazed about him with extreme benevolence.

"Perhaps you can shed a little light on a mystery, Doctor," I said.

"Mystery? What mystery? Don't tell me Madge has been watering the beer again!" He chuckled comfortably at his own joke.

"The very idea!" said Madge indignantly.

There was general laughter at this *riposte*, but I did not join in. I said to Killick: "I've got a letter here from a Mr. Hemingway who stayed here—or rather, booked a room— about three weeks ago."

Killick looked slightly bewildered, but Gibson added:

"You remember, Doctor; it was about the time when we had that bad storm."

"I remember the storm well enough," said Killick, "but I can't say that I remember a Mr. Hemingway."

"He arrived here," I said, "and he was shown to his room. Next morning he'd completely disappeared. Twenty-four hours later Norman got this letter with a five-pound note."

Killick examined the letter. "That was pretty generous," he remarked. Then he looked up in mild surprise. "Well," he said, "what's wrong with it?"

"Two things," I said. "In the first place, this mysterious Mr. Hemingway happens to be my ex-business partner, Harry Denston. Norman and Madge have both identified him from photographs."

"Oh?" murmured Dr. Killick non-committally.

"In the second place," I went on, "this letter wasn't written by Harry Denston. I know his handwriting as well as I know my own; I'm one of the very few people who can read it."

"Perhaps someone wrote the letter for him," suggested Madge brightly. "Perhaps he was too busy at the time. He *must* have been pretty busy to dash off like that, without saying a word to anyone."

"That's possible," I agreed. "Alternatively, he may not have known anything about the letter."

"I don't quite follow you, Mr. Frazer," Dr. Killick said.

"Look at it this way," I said. "Suppose Denston didn't want to leave here but was kidnapped . . ."

"Kidnapped?" echoed Madge in an awestruck voice.

Gibson drew a heavy breath. "Well, God bless my soul, Mr. Frazer!" he said.

Killick regarded me with indulgence. "Surely that's a bit far-fetched, my dear fellow."

"But *is* it so far-fetched, Doctor?" I said. "I don't think so. It fits the facts. Suddenly, in the middle of the night, this man disappears. Twenty-four hours later Norman receives a letter—supposedly sent by Hemingway—explaining why he vanished so suddenly. Naturally, Norman's perfectly satisfied—after all, a fiver for bed and breakfast is fair enough, particularly as he had neither bed *nor* breakfast. Right, Norman?"

"True enough, Mr. Frazer," said Gibson.

"Why should Norman be curious?" I went on. "He's made a fiver out of it—tax free."

"Too right," said Gibson with feeling.

Killick frowned in perplexity. "It seems logical enough," he admitted; "but kidnapping! Really, Mr. Frazer, I can't help feeling that you're jumping to rather melodramatic conclusions. Unless, of course, you've got a specific reason for believing that your friend really *was* kidnapped."

"No," I said, "I haven't any specific reason for thinking that."

"All the same," said Gibson thoughtfully, "it's pretty rum, whichever way you look at it."

Killick looked at his watch. "Well, I'm afraid I must be off. No rest for the wicked." He waved a hand in farewell and went out into the street.

"You're not very busy tonight," I remarked, looking round the deserted bar.

"We shall be in a few minutes," said Gibson. "They're all over at a darts match at the Crown. My regulars will all be back as soon as it's over."

"A nice chap, Dr. Killick," I commented.

Gibson picked up an ashtray and emptied it into the fire. "Oh aye," he said, "very popular in the village, is the doctor. And we don't take to strangers as a rule in these parts."

"But I thought he was a local man," I said.

Gibson shook his head. "Hardly that. You've got to have been here thirty years or more before you become a local. I shouldn't think Dr. Killick's been here much more than eighteen months. But he's a good chap for all that: always seems to be putting himself out to help folk. Must be pretty well off, I imagine."

Again the feeling came over me that Killick was a little too good to be true. "In what way does he help people?" I queried.

"Well, he looks after some of the old people like they was children. Then again, he's done a lot for Walters, the bloke we call Rembrandt."

"That's the artist I was hearing about earlier?"

Gibson nodded. "That's the one. Toughest looking chap I've ever seen; lives on a cabin cruiser out on the saltings."

I was silent for a moment. I was thinking of Will Truman's story about Rembrandt—the artist, drunkard, and trouble maker, who was so anxious to keep visitors away from his cabin cruiser. I wondered what strange bond of friendship existed between Dr. Killick, most conventional of general practitioners, and a man like Walters.

"If it hadn't been for the doctor," continued Gibson with relish, "I reckon Rembrandt would have gone inside by now. Bought some of his pictures, an' all—just to keep him going, like. 'Twasn't as if Rembrandt's pictures was any good, either, and I don't mind betting he spent all the money on booze. But the doctor's got a kind heart, see?"

Gibson's monologue was interrupted by the appearance of the nucleus of the Three Bells darts team, headed by Will Truman, whose verbosity seemed to be totally unimpaired.

"Now then, what about a bit o' service, Norman?" he demanded. "Don't want us all to go back to the Crown, do you?"

"If you can drink the swill they call beer there," said Gibson with a disdainful sniff, "you can buzz off now!"

I moved up the bar a little until I was standing next to Will Truman. "How did the match go?" I inquired.

"'Orrible!" said Truman disgustedly. "Some of the blokes wot calls 'emselves dart players 'ad a job 'itting the ruddy board. Charlie, 'ere, wanted a double-top to finish, an' wot does he do? Bloody near skewers an old geezer to the wall by 'is ear."

I laughed. "What about a drink?"

"I won't say no," said Will Truman. "I'll have a mild."

"I heard you talking about Rembrandt earlier on," I said. "It sounded like a good story. What happened?"

"Weren't a lot to it, really," said Truman. "We was just coming in when we 'eard this racket going on on board 'is boat. Thought 'e were 'aving a scrap wi' someone. Seems it weren't a fight at all, though, 'cos there were nobody there 'cept Owd Rembrandt—leastways, we couldn't see nobody. I reckon Rembrandt were a bit drunker than usual and breaking up the 'appy 'ome—Never 'eard such a blooming racket."

"This Rembrandt sounds quite a character," I remarked.

"He is that!" agreed Truman. "But I'm steering clear of 'im in future; I don't want to get meself slung in the drink. I got torpedoed twice in the ruddy Atlantic and that's enough for me, thank you."

I heard the telephone ringing and presently Gibson returned to the bar. "It's for you, Mr. Frazer," he announced.

"From London?" I asked.

"I don't think so. Sounds like a local call."

I put my glass on the bar and walked to the telephone. I said: "This is Tim Frazer . . ."

The voice on the other end was weak and tremulous, but I recognised it immediately. It said jerkily: "Tim, this is Harry . . . If you want to see me, I'll meet you in . . . about half an hour . . ."

"Where?" I demanded. This time I was going to tie him down to a definite time and place or know the reason why.

There was a pause and I thought I could hear a vague muttering at the other end. Then a voice spoke again; it sounded like Harry's, although I was not absolutely sure. The voice said: "At the jetty—near the Old Bell . . ." There was a buzz as the receiver was replaced.

I said desperately: "Harry, are you there?" But there was no answer. I wondered if the call could be traced, but gave up the idea. I put down the receiver and turned to Gibson.

"Where's the Old Bell?" I asked him.

He looked at me queerly for a moment. "That'll be the old ship's bell hanging down on the jetty," he said.

The jetty was deserted when I arrived there. The warehouses seemed to cast huge, eerie shadows over the large open space. I drove up and stopped outside a small stone building at the end of the jetty. Prominently displayed in front of this building was the bell, suspended from an old-fashioned iron wall-bracket.

On seeing the bell I moved over to it. I stopped underneath it and peered into the darkness: there was nothing in sight and a cold, clammy silence hung over the whole area. I shivered, not entirely from cold.

I lit a cigarette and looked at my watch in the flame of my lighter. Then I stiffened: I had noticed a very slight

movement in the shadow of one of the warehouses. I heard a
very faint shuffling sound, as if a man was shifting his weight
from one foot to the other. I stood absolutely motionless,
listening intently. Then I deliberately walked a short distance
from the small building and stood with my back to the warehouse. The silence was relieved only by the sound of the
wind coming in from the sea. I shivered again and admitted
freely to myself that I was scared as hell . . .

I looked round quickly, but saw nothing save the ghostly
outline of the warehouse. Then, faintly but quite audibly,
I heard a soft metallic click . . .

Some instinct prompted me to lean over sideways and
this undoubtedly saved my life. A man lunged at me from
behind and I felt a knife rip through the side of my raincoat.
I lashed out with my right fist and connected with the man's
cheekbone. He cursed horribly and I knew that voice at
once—it was the man who had called himself Lester. With an
upward stroke he slashed at my arm, but I managed to get
a grip on his wrist.

We swayed backwards and forwards and I could hear
Lester mouthing obscenities. He jerked his right knee up,
but I anticipated the move and, catching Lester's ankle,
threw him sideways. He fell heavily on the cobblestones.

But he had retained his hold on the knife. This time he
came at me head down and slashed at my face. I ducked in
the nick of time and seized Lester's knife hand, at the same
time driving my other fist into his midriff. I weigh a good
thirteen stone and most of it was behind that punch. I
almost heard the breath going out of Lester and the knife
fell to the ground with a clatter.

But he wasn't finished yet. He made a dive for the knife,
and I kicked it towards the edge of the jetty. Lester went
after it, but I dived for his legs in a rugger tackle before he

could reach it. I hauled him to his feet and gave him a clean uppercut right on the point of the jaw.

Lester let out a thin squeal like a trapped rabbit as my hands fastened on his throat. He kicked out desperately and caught me squarely on the knee-cap, but I still managed to hold on to him. Seizing him by his coat collar I swung him round and rocked him to his heels with a smashing right-hander to the mouth.

Lester recoiled, but came for me again. By this time we were on the extreme edge of the jetty. Below us the sea swirled blackly. Snarling like an animal, Lester wrapped both arms round my waist. I broke from his hold and seized him by the throat again; then my grip relaxed as Lester bit into the back of my hand.

I knew that he was considerably younger and probably fitter than I, and my only chance was to finish him with a knock-out punch. Summoning up my last ounce of strength —and I hadn't a lot left—I drove a punch at Lester's face. He suddenly threw up his arms, screamed shrilly, and vanished into the blackness below.

Breathing hard, staggering a couple of paces, and clutching my stomach, I looked down into the sea. Waves of pain and nausea swept over me. I put my hand up to my face and tasted warm blood.

I looked down at the sea again. The waves battered against the jetty. Then I kicked the knife after Lester and walked unsteadily back to my car . . .

CHAPTER FOURTEEN

I SLEPT late the next morning and unsettled Madge somewhat by refusing a cup of tea when she appeared with it at eight o'clock.

I went down to the bar at ten thirty and made a suitable apology to Madge. Norman Gibson raised his eyebrows slightly when I ordered a double whisky and soda instead of breakfast.

I took my drink to a table by the window and sat down gingerly. My head ached abominably and there was a dull, throbbing pain in my knee. I had repaired most of the damage to my hand, but Lester's teeth marks seemed to be leering at me. My face was unmarked, however, which was just as well: I didn't want Norman Gibson or Madge, both insatiable seekers after knowledge, to ask too many questions at this stage.

I don't usually drink double whiskies at ten thirty a.m., but on this particular morning it seemed the most natural thing in the world. As I drank, I tried to make some coherent plan.

Lester was dead and I had killed him: there did not seem much point in thinking about him in terms of flesh and blood. If and when his body was recovered Ross would take care of that. I felt no remorse about killing Lester and in any event it had been a clear case of self-defence. If Lester had not gone into the sea he would very definitely have killed me.

I was, however, no nearer to finding Harry, although it

was now quite clear that he was somewhere in Henton. There remained Walters—or Rembrandt. However drunk he might be, I could hardly believe Will Truman's story that he had been breaking up a costly cabin cruiser just for the fun of it.

I had another drink in the bar and then went out. The cold air was refreshing and my head started to clear. A visit to Rembrandt was obviously indicated. From what I had heard, he was likely to be an even tougher proposition than Lester, and I didn't look forward to another free-for-all.

I remembered Ross saying that some of his men would be in Henton, and I found this knowledge as comforting as the bulge of the ·32 automatic through my raincoat. To substantiate Ross's promise a fisherman crossed the street and stood a few yards from me, busily rolling a cigarette.

As I came up to him I saw that he was a middle-aged man wearing a rough blue jersey and thigh-length rubber boots. He looked up and down the street and then said quietly: "Rembrandt's cabin cruiser is moored down at the quay. When you see Rembrandt tell him that you're an art dealer on the lookout for pictures for your new gallery. You've seen a picture of his—it's of a shopping basket on a table— and you thought it was pretty good. You've been told about Rembrandt by Henry Frindale. You'd better repeat that back to me."

He need not have worried; I have the sort of memory that readily assimilates such details. The fisherman nodded and then spat accurately on the cobbled street. He said: "Good luck to you." Then he turned abruptly on his heel and headed for the Crown.

The cabin cruiser was a long, slim, powerful looking craft, obviously capable of considerable speed. I stood on the quayside, looking at it for a moment. Presently a man came up on deck and emptied a bucket over the side.

Obviously this was Rembrandt. He lit a pipe and stood leaning over the rail. I wondered whether I should prove as convincing as an art dealer as I had apparently been in the guise of a Scotland Yard detective. Ross's organisation was pretty good, I thought: naturally the sensible approach to Walters was either through his pictures or the offer of a bottle of whisky. I decided that I was not in the mood to stand him a drink.

I walked casually up the gangplank and stepped on to the deck. I could see that Norman Gibson's description of Rembrandt was in no way exaggerated. He stood at least six feet five inches tall and was broad in proportion. His black hair grew in profusion on his bullet head and most of his face was obscured by a tangled and unkempt beard. When he heard me approach he swung round abruptly and regarded me with a glare that was unmistakably hostile.

Standing at the top of the gangway, with his arms folded, he blocked my approach in no uncertain manner. "What the hell are you after?" he rasped. "This boat is private property." His lips were drawn back, there was a wild look in his eyes, and the smell of whisky on his breath brought back a resurgence of my former nausea.

"Are you Mr. Walters?" I inquired politely.

"That's me. What the bloody hell do you want?"

"My name's Clifton," I explained. "I'm an art dealer."

"Clifton?" said Walters suspiciously. "I've never heard of you."

"That's hardly surprising," I said casually. "I hadn't heard of you until a fortnight ago."

"So what?" said Walters offensively.

"I've been in New York for the past four years," I said.

"Now I'm opening a gallery in New Bond Street and I'm looking for some good pictures. I think we may be able to do business together."

Walters glared at me through bloodshot eyes. "Who told you to come here? Who told you about me?"

"You're a very suspicious individual," I said pleasantly. "If you're not interested in selling your work, then just say so and I'll go elsewhere."

"You haven't answered my question," he grated.

I raised my eyebrows. "What was your question?"

Walters' small eyes narrowed to the merest slits. "I asked you who told you about me?"

Very deliberately I turned my back on him. "Forget it, my dear fellow," I said with dignity. "I can't waste my time on temperamental painters, however brilliant they may be."

Walters grabbed my arm and swung me round to face him. "Answer my question!" he barked.

Displaying confidence that I was very far from feeling, I said: "Henry Frindale told me about you. I saw a picture of yours in his gallery. I liked it and he told me where I could find you. Does that satisfy you, Mr. Walters?"

"What was the picture?"

"It was a shopping basket on a kitchen table."

Walters bared his discoloured teeth in a smile. "I should bloody well think you did like it," he said. "It's the best picture you've seen in years—or are likely to." Walters evidently had a high opinion of his artistic ability.

"A slight overstatement," I said easily, "although I must admit that it has a certain merit."

Walters scowled at me belligerently. "I've just finished a picture that beats anything you've seen anywhere in America."

"Better than the shopping basket on the table?"

He spat expressively into the sea.

"Splendid!" I said with professional enthusiasm. "Supposing you let the picture speak for itself?"

But it seemed that I had not allayed all his suspicions. "You did say you know Henry Frindale, didn't you?"

"Of course I know him," I said with a trace of impatience. "I know all the dealers. I suppose you wouldn't like me to call back later with a letter of introduction?"

"Don't be a bloody fool," said Walters.

"Well, then," I said amicably, "I suggest you let me see the picture. Who knows? We may be wasting my time as well as yours."

Walters glared at me and then turned towards the companionway. "I'll fetch it," he said shortly.

He shuffled off down the companionway and I looked round the deck. I moved cautiously towards the superstructure of the cabin. Suddenly I stopped, and looked up; a somewhat dilapidated life-belt had caught my eye. Inscribed on this life-belt in black letters was the word:

ANYA

At that moment everything fell into place in my mind. I remembered the dying Russian sailor who had muttered "Anya" over and over again; I recalled the shock of discovering that the little girl at Edwards' cottage was also, incredibly, called Anya. It was now apparent that I was on very dangerous territory.

I tiptoed round to a porthole and by bending down could see into the cabin. Walters was rummaging among a disordered array of canvases which were untidily stacked against one of the walls. Standing with his back to me was a portly figure that was unmistakably Dr. Killick.

M

There was a man lying on the bunk, apparently unconscious. I drew in my breath sharply as I looked at his face. It was Harry Denston . . .

A huge, purplish bruise stretched from his right cheekbone to the edge of his mouth. His upper lip was swollen to almost twice its normal size and there was an ugly cut over his right eye which was half closed. There were traces of dried blood under his nostrils. His appearance explained the racket that Will Truman had heard.

Killick turned round and I hastily backed away from the porthole. Then I realised that Killick was leaving the cabin to come up on deck and that it would be impossible to avoid him.

When he saw me Killick smiled broadly. "Why, Mr. Frazer," he said genially, "what on earth are you doing here?"

He was still the friendly, somewhat easy going doctor whom I had known in The Three Bells, to all outward appearance. I regarded him warily and kept my right hand on the revolver in my pocket.

"What's rather more to the point, Doctor," I said grimly, "is what *you're* doing here."

Killick waved a hand towards the cabin. "I have a patient on board," he said airily. "He's delirious, poor chap. Very sad case altogether."

"I'm sure it is," I said. "Who's your patient?"

"He's a relation of Rembrandt's," said Killick affably. "Forgive me, I mean Walters, of course. But you don't know him, do you? A most entertaining fellow, if a little eccentric. He's an artist, you know."

"And you," I said dispassionately, "are a damned liar."

I saw Killick's eyes narrow, but his mouth fell open in perfectly feigned surprise. "I beg your pardon, Mr. Frazer?"

"I said you're a damned liar," I repeated. "Your patient,

as you call him, isn't a relation of Rembrandt's. He's Harry Denston."

Killick gave a gentle sigh. "Harry Denston? My dear fellow, you seem to have that name on the brain." He stepped forward to intercept me as I moved towards the companionway, then called out sharply: "Where d'you think you're going?"

"I'll give you three guesses," I said.

"My patient can't be disturbed," protested Killick. "I forbid you to go down there, d'you understand?"

"Your patient is Harry Denston," I said. I produced the automatic and pointed it straight at Killick's stomach. "Now, cut out the bluff and tell your tame muscle man to bring him up on deck."

"Are you threatening me?"

"Yes, I'm threatening you," I said. "Do as I say, Killick. Tell Rembrandt to bring Harry Denston up here and look sharp about it."

Killick seemed about to renew his protest, but I made a threatening movement with the gun.

"Fetch Denston," I repeated.

Killick shrugged his shoulders. He said: "Don't you think you're being rather stupid about this?"

"I don't think so," I said. "You don't imagine I'm on my own do you?"

Killick looked towards the quayside. A police car had just drawn up and a grey Jaguar. Four uniformed policemen got out of the police car and stood watching the *Anya* as if awaiting orders. Among the plain-clothes men I noticed the bulky figure of John Caxton.

Killick looked round despairingly. I said: "You can swim for it if you like, Killick, but I don't think you'll get far."

Moving remarkably quickly for a man of his comfortable

build Killick made a dash for the gangplank. He stepped on to the quay and sprinted towards a side street.

I was right. The men in uniform at once converged upon him.

Caxton and two other men came aboard the *Anya*. To the accompaniment of some very strong language Walters was handcuffed and led away. Caxton and I went below to the cabin.

Harry Denston had propped himself up against the dirty pillow on the bunk. His battered lips parted in the grin that I knew so well. Whatever happened, I thought, they couldn't make Harry talk. He said weakly: "Hello, Tim. I'm afraid I've been a bit of a bloody nuisance."

I smiled at him; there was nothing else I could do. It had always been the same—Harry produced that infectious grin and there was no resisting it.

"You can say that again." I said.

"The luck had to run out some time," he murmured.

Caxton produced a hip flask and opened it. "Have a drink, Denston," he said. "You can talk later—you've got all the time in the world now . . ."

CHAPTER FIFTEEN

WAITING for my visitor, I tried to review the latest developments. I had just returned from the hospital where Ruth Edwards was making a steady recovery. Unfortunately, it had been difficult to get her to talk. I had imagined she might have been able to enlighten me as to Lester's importance in the scheme of things, but she insisted that she only knew of him by name and was unacquainted with his activities.

She had, however, proved rather more helpful on the question of Dr. Killick, though she claimed that he had been dragged into the affair and was not nearly as sinister as might at first appear. I told her that Killick had confessed to his full share in the recent happenings, but had maintained that he was ignorant of the identity of the man from whom he took his instructions. He tried to give the impression that it had been one of the mysterious Russians, but I had told him quite frankly I did not believe him.

Ruth Edwards had proved equally obstinate, and it is not easy to extract information from a woman who is only recently off the danger list. Once or twice I noticed the nurse giving me a warning look, but I had to go on. And in the end Ruth Edwards had told me what I wanted to know.

Feeling a reaction to this experience, I had poured myself a stiff whisky, and was just finishing it when the doorbell rang. My visitor had arrived.

It was Donald Edwards, shabby and diffident as always.

"Come along in, Mr. Edwards," I said hospitably. "It was nice of you to call."

I took his threadbare raincoat and hung it on a peg in the hall. We went into the drawing-room together.

"How's your wife?" I said. "What's the latest news?" Though, of course, I knew the answer.

Edwards, apparently more relaxed than I had ever seen him, sat down. "She's off the danger list now," he said. "They say she should be up and about in four or five weeks." He produced a tired smile. "I must say, I shall be very relieved when she comes home; a daily woman is a poor substitute."

"I'm delighted to hear that she's better," I said. I sat down opposite Edwards. "I expect you're wondering why I asked you to call."

"Well, I was a little puzzled, I must confess," he said.

I settled myself more comfortably in my chair. "I want to tell you a story, Mr. Edwards, that I feel sure will interest you: it concerns the *North Star*." I was watching him carefully, but he registered only polite wonderment. "It's not a very pretty story," I went on, "but I think you'll be intrigued by it."

Edwards looked at his watch. "I'm afraid I haven't a great deal of time," he said apologetically.

"You've time enough for this," I said. "It also concerns a man called Harry Denston who is a friend of mine."

"Harry Denston?" mused Edwards. "I seem to have heard that name before."

"You have indeed," I said. "You used the *North Star* as a stepping stone to get to know Harry and to gain his confidence. He told you that he'd just bought some maritime prints. You were interested and he showed them to you." I picked up the print of the *North Star* from the table. "This was one of them."

"I think there must be some mistake," said Edwards in

tones of mild reproof. "The first time I saw this print was when you brought it to the cottage"—his smile was a study in confused innocence—"and I certainly don't know this friend of yours—what's his name again?"

"Harry Denston."

Edwards shook his head regretfully. He conveyed the impression that he was only too anxious to help. "I'm afraid that's just a name to me, Mr. Frazer. I don't know him."

"I think you do," I persisted quietly. "You see, I have this story on the very best authority."

"Whose authority?"

"Your brother-in-law, Dr. Killick's," I said deliberately. "Anya's father."

I noticed that his eyes were no longer blinking short-sightedly, but were cold and watchful. Edwards said quietly: "Go on, Mr. Frazer. I'm beginning to find this quite interesting."

"You'll find it even more interesting in a minute," I said. "You built a model of the *North Star* for Harry, using this print as a guide. When you got to know Harry better, and discovered that he was in financial difficulties, you offered him money to photograph a certain formula."

I waited for him to make some comment but he only shook his head.

"This formula," I went on, "belonged to an acquaintance of Harry's, a man called John Sinclair White. Harry took the money and did what you wanted. But he didn't play it straight, Mr. Edwards. He double-crossed you and gave you a microfilm containing false information."

"This is all very interesting, Mr. Frazer," said Edwards. His voice was imperturbable, but his eyes were not still for a second.

"I'm glad you think so," I said. "It gets even more intriguing."

Edwards inclined his head slightly and waited for me to continue.

"Harry then contacted an East German organisation and arranged to meet their representative, a man called Anstrov, at Henton. You heard about this and immediately informed them that Denston hadn't got the formula and that *you* were the man to contact. Anstrov agreed to meet you on Killick's cabin cruiser, which was named *Anya* after his daughter." I paused to allow this to sink in.

Edwards shook his head sadly. "I can only assume, Mr. Frazer," he said, "that the strain of your recent activities has in some way unsettled you."

"It's unsettled me considerably," I said grimly, "and I think what I'm going to say may unsettle you a little too. *You* know what happened: there was a shipwreck and Anstrov died. Before he died he mentioned the name 'Anya'. We know now, of course, that he was referring to the boat and not to Killick's daughter."

"These are very serious charges, Mr. Frazer," remarked Edwards.

"They're intended to be." I stood with my back to the fireplace, never taking my eyes off Edwards for an instant. "You kidnapped Denston and tried to make him talk, but all you could get out of him was the admission that the microfilm you wanted was in the *North Star*. Then you sent your friend Lester—the *late* Lester, I should say—to get the model from Harry's flat." I smiled reminiscently. "An unpleasant character, Lester. I had to kill him."

Edwards looked startled. "You admit you killed him?" he said involuntarily.

"If I hadn't," I said, "he would have undoubtedly killed

me. We had an argument and he—fell into the sea. I imagine that he's still there. However, I'm straying from the point a little. When Lester arrived at Harry's flat he saw Crombie leaving with the model. Lester followed Crombie back here, murdered him, and took the model when I was safely out of the way."

"But the film wasn't in the model!" Edwards blurted out.

"No it wasn't," I said. "But when Harry told you it was in the *North Star* he was telling the truth. *The film was in the* North Star, *but not in the model.*"

Edwards' face was blank and expressionless. I looked at him quickly and then picked up the print again. I put it face down on the table. Then I removed the backing and took out an envelope from which I extracted a length of film.

"You were so convinced that Harry meant the model," I said, "that it never occurred to you to *look in the print.*"

Edwards rose to his feet. With a quick movement he thrust his hand into his jacket pocket; when it came out it held a small, foreign-looking automatic revolver. He was breathing quickly and obviously deciding on a plan for a quick getaway.

I said: "It may interest you to know, Mr. Edwards, that we have had an audience." I jerked my head towards the bedroom door. "That gun doesn't even amuse me."

The bedroom door then opened to reveal John Caxton; his huge bulk seemed to fill the room with massive invincibility. He held a revolver in his hand.

"This is the end of the line, Edwards," Caxton said in a voice that sounded almost bored. "Put that gun away . . ."

CHAPTER SIXTEEN

Ross surveyed me benevolently from behind his ornate desk. He said: "Well, that's that. Everything seems to have wound up very nicely. Though I'm afraid you had rather a troublesome time." He might have been the managing director of a big business house commiserating with an executive who had been involved in a tricky deal.

"There were certainly some tight corners," I agreed.

"In this department," said Ross in measured tones, "we know only too well, that appearances can be cruelly deceptive; things are hardly ever what they seem. That applies to people as well." He put a cigarette in his mouth and lit it with a desk lighter. "Edwards certainly looked the part of a meek little man whose sole interest in life was making models of ships."

"He had me fooled at first," I admitted ruefully.

"Naturally," said Ross. "He had studied his part for quite a long time and he deceived almost everyone. He was also indirectly responsible for the deaths of Crombie and Tupper. Incidentally, did Edwards find out about that note his wife sent you? Is that why he tried to kill her?"

"No," I said. "He heard her talking to me on the telephone and thought I was doing a private deal with her over the film."

"I see," said Ross thoughtfully. He blew a ruminative cloud of smoke towards the ceiling. "Then he thought *you* had the film?"

"Yes, he jumped to the conclusion that Harry might have

passed it on to me. The irony of the situation is that I actually did have it when I had the print, but I didn't know it."

Ross nodded. "Obviously, Edwards didn't know which way to turn. First he thought it might be in Harry Denston's car; then he concentrated on the model . . ."

"That's why they wanted the photograph so badly," I broke in. "When they found that the film wasn't in Harry's model they thought there might be another model of the *North Star* in existence. A photograph would have shown Edwards any little differences."

"I understand you saw Mrs. Edwards this morning?"

"Yes," I said. "She explained about the note. Apparently *two* men came over from East Germany."

"Anstrov and Nikiyan," said Ross. "Anstrov was known to be the important man on the mission and Nikiyan his assistant. In case of any funny business they changed names and identities. It was Nikiyan who died."

"And Anstrov?"

"He left for Berlin this morning."

"You mean—you let him go?"

"Yes."

"Why?"

Ross got up from his desk and walked over to the mantelpiece. He stood with his back to the fireplace, smoking composedly. "If we'd picked him up." he said, "there would have been complications. We like to avoid complications as much as possible. Our job was to see that when Anstrov did leave he left empty handed. He did."

"And what happens to Harry Denston?" I asked.

"Frankly, I don't know about that," said Ross. "You see, it's out of my hands. Harry Denston is the Home Secretary's headache now. I'm very much more concerned with what happens to *you*."

"What do you mean?" I asked.

"What are you going to do, now that this business is over?"

I shrugged. "I don't know," I said vaguely. "I'd half decided to go abroad—Australia or somewhere."

Ross looked at me keenly. "How would you like to work for me?"

"You mean permanently? Join your department?"

"That's just what I mean. I'm offering you Crombie's job."

There was a brief silence between us. Ross continued to eye me speculatively.

For the first time since I had known him Ross's voice sounded faintly hesitant. He said: "This is all slightly embarrassing. I'm not trying to influence you, one way or the other. But the fact remains that you've done a damned fine job. There'll be other assignments; possibly easier than this one, possibly even more difficult. It's entirely up to you." He looked out of the window.

After a long pause I said: "Tell me about the next job, Mr. Ross . . ."